The Killer's Daughter

The Killer's Daughter

VIVIAN OLDAKER

ANDERSEN PRESS • LONDON

First published in 2009 by
Andersen Press Limited
20 Vauxhall Bridge Road
London SW1V 2SA

www.andersenpress.co.uk

British Library Cataloguing in Publication Data available.

ISBN 978 184 270 814 9

Typeset by FiSH Books Ltd, Enfield, Middx.
Printed and bound in Great Britain by
CPI Bookmarque, Croydon CR0 4TD

For Pete. (1956–2001). We made it, bro.

PROLOGUE

'At what time,' said the policeman, 'did you find the body?'

'I don't wear a watch,' Costas said, 'but the sun was just coming up over the black hill.'

He sipped the strong, black coffee and shivered. The air conditioning in the police station was fierce.

'Tell me about it again,' the policeman said. 'You weren't making a lot of sense before.'

Costas sighed. The coffee wasn't bad but really, he had to get out of here as quickly as possible.

'Try to stick to the point this time.' The policeman started the recording device.

'Go on,' he said.

'OK, then. I was on the beach, it was sunrise. The old lady was lying across the rocks, like she was posing, or maybe sunbathing – except it was too early for that. She was face down, her feet were in a rock pool, one shoe missing, her arms spread wide, like this.'

Costas gestured. The policeman decided to let it go – you couldn't record a gesture but he didn't want to interrupt the flow.

'So I went closer,' Costas continued. 'I had my camera with me. I am, as you know, a photographer, which is why I was down on the beach so early, because I wanted to get some pretty shots of the sunrise over the island. Anyway, I thought it would be a good idea to photograph the lady – maybe to be of help to the police. I focused my camera on the side of her head. It was at an angle, so I could see her closed eye, her nose and some of her mouth. It might not be a crime scene, but I thought I should take the photos, to help the police.'

1

'You said that already,' said the policeman. 'If only everyone was as public-spirited – please continue.'

'Perhaps she killed herself... old people today are often lonely. In her hand was some green stuff from the bushes.'

'Myrtle.'

'If you say so – anyway she maybe killed herself or maybe fell – who knows?'

The policeman ignored this. 'And did you know who she was?'

'No. I had an idea that I'd maybe seen her before, but I didn't recognise her. But I was almost certain she wasn't Greek.'

'Why?'

'She looked about eighty. No black dress, an expensive-looking white trouser suit. She was wearing a blonde wig, with many curls.'

'How did you know it was a wig?'

'Easy, it wasn't on her head properly, perhaps it got dislodged when she fell; underneath I could see a patch of very short grey hair.'

'And then what?'

'I was going to call the police, but then I thought maybe I should see if she had any identification.'

'Interfering with the scene,' the policeman said.

'I did what I thought best,' Costas said, defensively. 'After all, if I hadn't come along just then she might have lain there for hours.'

'Go on.'

'I reached into her pockets – I had to lift her shoulder slightly – there was a ten-euro note and some change in one, a handkerchief in the other and then...'

'And then?'

'Little red streams came towards me. From where I'd raised her, they made her jacket pink... blood. I hate the sight of blood. She tried to claw my face with her free hand. "Dino," she said. "Dino." I was so shocked I dropped my camera. It bounced on a rock and into the sand – ruined. Then I pressed 100 on my phone and I told them to send an ambulance. In the end I had to go in the ambulance, I was so shocked. I sat next to the driver. They said she was dead, but I couldn't be sure, after that.'

'And did she say anything else, before the ambulance arrived?'

Costas shrugged. 'Her last word on this earth was "sand". ' He tapped the side of his head with his forefinger, the international symbol for madness.

'I wonder why she said that...' the policeman said, thoughtfully.

'Who knows? There was a lot of sand around.'

'Sure. And is there anything else you can tell us, Costas?'

'Not a thing. I've told you everything.'

'If you do remember anything else, just phone me.' He handed Costas a card.

'I will. At the moment I need a stiff drink...it was horrible, horrible, especially for a sensitive man like myself.'

The policeman nodded sympathetically. Costas-the-Photographer was not actually a man noted for his sensitive nature; but such an event would be a shock to anyone.

Costas exited the police station into the bright sunshine and put on his shades. He thought he'd done a good job of lying to the police. Of course he'd known the identity of the victim. But he had nothing to worry about now – except the price of a new camera.

CHAPTER ONE

The peace of the countryside? Just try getting a good night's sleep in the place.

The night before term starts: a full moon to lighten my darkness, a zillion owls parked in the trees, dozens of dogs taking part in the Loudest Bark competition; assorted screaming cats – plus sundry other sounds of the squeaking, creaking and scratching variety – rats? Please, not rats. As a grand finale, around 4.00 a.m., I swear I hear a coyote.

So here I am, first day at school for the new kid in town – or rather, in country. Everyone will be looking at me, judging me. Welcome to the Wilds of Wessex.

The shoes are OK. I persuaded Jan to let me have them even though the school brochure says plain, flat black. 'No one takes any notice of that,' I said. (I knew they wouldn't.)

But I'm not pleased to see that they all wear ties and – can you believe it? – blazers! Not just blazers but green blazers. How sad is that? Mine stays in my bag until the moment I walk through those shiny black gates and it goes right back in there the second the bell rings and I'm out the door; at 4.05 precisely.

I'm having to repeat Year 10 – 'verily, this doth sucketh,' as my old friend Will Shakespeare might have said if they'd had Year 10 in Tudor times. But I missed so much last year what with the court case and everything that I don't have a lot of choice. We had to move here. Jan said Dad wasn't coping in Wandsworth and I could see that the bucolic lifestyle might suit him better.

Bucolic. I'm the only one to raise my hand in English when

4

Miss Tidesman asks if anyone knows what it means. Unless you count the tall boy with the floppy brown hair and big teeth who says: 'Does it mean: addicted to buc?' (Big laughs – they're obviously easily amused round these parts.) It is just so weird being at school with boys. My last seat of learning was a male-free zone, except for a couple of fossilised teachers who hardly qualified.

Not that I'm looking for a boyfriend. Actually I've never had one, partly because in Wandsworth I always hung around with Surrinder, my best mate, for whom boys were strictly off-limits. And I suppose the other reason is, if I'm honest, because no one I'd fancy would fancy me.

My ideal guy would be someone like John Travolta – actually it would be John Travolta. Maybe not so much John as he is now – he's still the coolest, most charismatic actor on the planet but even I have to admit he's maybe a little old for me. My absolute favourite John used to be Danny Zuko in *Grease*, followed by Tony Manero in *Saturday Night Fever*. Now that I'm more mature, Ideal John is Chili Palmer in *Get Shorty*; Sean Archer in *Face/Off*; Vic Deakins in *Broken Arrow*; and, on my wild days, Vincent Vega in *Pulp Fiction*... I would have killed to be Uma Thurman during that dance.

There have of course been turkeys of the juiciest kind in John's long and glorious career. I could have happily lived without ever seeing him as Woody Stevens in *Wild Hogs*. Travolta hasn't always soared on celluloid... Is there a single major Hollywood player who has? But when he's in the right movie with the right script and the right director, John truly flies.

Surrinder says I'm crazy and, if I have to lust after celebs, why not someone more appropriate, like Jake or Zac or Orlando? There are times when I worry about Surrinder's sanity. I should say: 'used to worry'. Surrinder is no longer my concern, of course.

We used to be best friends – two freaky weirdo geek girls in a school of conformists. We belonged to no tribe except our own.

Somehow though, I can't quite see John and me strolling off into the sunset together – especially now I've moved away from the Steaming Metropolis to Hicksville. The chances of my meeting John and of our finding True Love together (which were, admittedly, never that great) are now absolutely zero.

Miss Tidesman seems OK. She says we'll be doing some Thomas Hardy – he came from around these parts – and has anyone read any of his stuff? This time I keep my hand firmly by my side. I've read *Far from the MC* and *The Mayor of Casterbridge* but, hey, let's not get ourselves a reputation as Little Miss Boffin on day one.

I think I'll make bucolic my Word of the Week. I always had a W of the W when we lived in civilisation; it's a tradition I've decided to keep.

Baked potato with tuna and salad for lunch (what a sensible child). I sit next to two girls from my tutor group – Soph and Stace. They're quite friendly.

'You're Emma X – something – we saw your name on the register.'

'That's me.'

'Funny surname – how d'you say it?'

'Eggsenos – but most people say Zen-oss, spelled X E N O S; it's Greek.'

'You Greek?'

'Half. My dad's Greek.'

'You don't look Greek.'

I know. My hair's light brown, my eyes are grey and I've got freckles. I suppose I must take after my mum, but as she died when I was three and Dad has only a couple of faded photos in his sock drawer, I'll probably never know.

I'd rather be like my dad – apart from the beard of course. It'd be great to have dark hair and big brown eyes and olive skin – to look mysterious and interesting – or at least, less ordinary.

Soph and Stace ask me about my last school and seem impressed when I tell them it was in London. They tell me about the teachers I haven't met yet; about their boyfriends; about Soph's gran's cataract operation; about the busted Tampax machine in the girls' loo that no one wants to tell the caretaker about because it's tooo embarrassing; about Stace's Doberman's new puppies; about Soph's little brother Anthony who's a right pain; about foods to avoid in the canteen (apparently the lasagne looks and tastes like sick); about the new school swimming pool which was opened (and paid for) by a soap star who's an ex-pupil ... All this before the bell goes for afternoon registration.

CHAPTER TWO

When I get home Dad's upstairs with a migraine. He's finding it a big effort setting up his new workshop in the barn. Maybe he should get one of those Feng Shui people to check out the energy flows or something. It's hard for him, being such a perfectionist. But I suppose if he wasn't he might not have what it takes to make his beautiful jewellery. All of his pieces have a little label attached: Di-Xen. That stands for Dionysus Xenos.

Jan is in the middle of major aggravation with the next-door neighbour, Mrs Denny. Mrs Denny looks at me like I'm some rare and exotic species – probably poisonous. It seems the neighbours know all about Dad. She says she hopes we'll have the decency to keep ourselves to ourselves, if Jan knows what she means. Jan says she understands her perfectly, thank you, and that none of us has the slightest intention of trying to make friends with a bunch of rural bigots. Also that Dad was found not guilty… Quick as a flash, Mrs Denny says not guilty isn't the same as innocent and 'everyone knows there's no smoke without fire'.

Jan says she'd be obliged if Mrs Denny would sod off. Mrs Denny does so. I make Jan a cup of tea and she lights a cigarette – for once I don't give her a hard time about it. How did Mrs Denny find out so quickly about Dad? How many other people know?

Dad and Jan have been together a long time – I can't really remember life before Jan. She used to be a nurse. Nowadays she mostly just looks after Dad or reads books; sometimes she paints abstracts – at the moment she's going through a red stage; there are scarlet, maroon, crimson and blood-coloured canvases everywhere. Some of them look like crime scenes.

I was going to practise my saxophone. Somehow I don't feel like it now. This house is big – much more space than our old one, so I don't suppose I'd disturb Dad. But Mrs Denny and her spiteful little eyes have put me off playing for now.

My new school has an orchestra – maybe I'll try to get into that, at least it would make me practice. Though I don't suppose I'll be into whatever music they do. What I like best is jazz sax: John Coltrane, Andy Sheppard, Brandon Fields, Courtney Pine.

Jan told Mrs Denny that none of us wants to make friends but, actually, I wouldn't mind. I thought this was supposed to be a fresh start. I'm fed up with having no one to talk to. Surrinder's parents forbade her to speak to me once Dad's case came up. She's a very obedient girl. It's all right for Dad and Jan – at least they have each other.

Jan said we were lucky to get this house, though being able to pay cash certainly helped. It's detached; she reckons it was built about a hundred years ago. There are big, old-fashioned sash windows in the main rooms. The kitchen opens out on to a yard with a creaky old spiders' paradise of a shed in the corner. There's a path that leads from some French windows in the living room to a small area of garden and Dad's barn/workshop which is, apparently, much older than the house. We've got four bedrooms now – there were only two in our Wandsworth house, which was in the middle of a terrace with a front door that opened onto the street, putting you instantly in the middle of things.

My new bedroom is massive. What's really good is that they've let me have a big TV and a DVD and a sound system and a brand new PC in here. Dad wasn't too sure about all the 'appliances', as he calls them.

'Why does she need to watch telly alone? It isn't healthy.'

9

Jan told him teenagers need their own space. I wasn't about to argue – though she never said that when we lived in Wandsworth. They won't let me have what Jan calls unfettered internet access here though, which sucks, big time. It's because when we were in Wandsworth I used to occasionally visit chatrooms to talk about John Travolta – well, quite a lot actually. Dad said I was becoming obsessive, which was completely unfair. Jan said when she was my age she used to fantasise about an actor called Gene Kelly and everyone thought she was an oddball, but they didn't have chatrooms in those days. I said, 'No kidding? Did they even have electricity?' Dad told me not to be cheeky.

Dad says if he thinks I'm spending too much time alone in my room, he'll take all my stuff away. But how would he know, since he spends nearly all his time in his room?

I change into my black T-shirt and jeans, plus a necklace that Dad made especially for me. It's silver with a beautiful blue stone called lapis lazuli, which Dad always says sounds more like a flower than a gemstone. It looks a bit like an eye and it's supposed to keep away Evil – a pity I wasn't wearing it when Mrs Denny was polluting the atmosphere. I polish it with my thumb while I tackle my first ever piece of maths homework from Hillingbury High.

Hillingbury High is the school that Time forgot. It has a very strict anti-jewellery policy. At least at my old school I could wear some of Dad's earrings – well, the studs anyway. I've got thirty-two pairs made by Dad plus a few Indian ones from Southall where Surrinder's aunt lives. The ones by Dad are the best though, because they're unique. He supplies some seriously expensive shops in London and New York. I'm going to help him set up a website to sell direct...soon; when he's settled in here.

I love jewellery. But my favourite piece wasn't actually made by Dad. It's an old antique ruby ring that my Grandma Susie gave me when I was a baby. She had a thing about antique rings. I just have this one – which is much too big for me. I don't know where the rest went to after she was killed.

The next day we have a talk from the head teacher, Mr Hampton. He tells us that the next two years will be crucial if we are all to fulfil our potential. That it is time to put away childish things and grasp the nettle of study with both hands.

The boy with the big teeth says 'ouch' rather too loudly and Hampton glares at him. I think he (the boy, not Mr Hampton) is called Bruce. Even though he plays about a lot he's a brainiac. He's already passed GCSE Maths A-star, so Stace says.

When I get home I give Jan a note about Parents' Evening. Jan groans and says, do she and Dad have to go? I say it isn't important. Jan says she's thinking of taking Dad away for a long weekend – the move has exhausted them both. Will I be OK on my own? Suddenly I feel like a toddler and very scared, but I just shrug and say of course, I'll be fine – especially if I can rent a DVD or three. Jan says that's reasonable, but I must promise not to have any parties while they're gone. Like, who would I invite? I say to Jan that people aren't exactly queuing up to be friends with me.

That's the problem with starting a new school in Year 10 – friendships got sorted long ago in Year 7 – or, with this bunch of carrot-crunchers, maybe even earlier. Probably most of them went to playgroup or nursery together.

Hillingbury High is populated by more or less the same tribes that inhabited my last school landscape – Chavs, Emos, Townies, Goths, Hippies, Skaters, Populars, Boffs, Metalheads, Wiggers. There don't seem to be many Gangstas. There aren't many non-white faces. I expect I'll discover a uniquely rural tribe soon – Wurzels, perhaps.

Jan says it must be tough for me, but that I should try not to be prejudiced against the locals just because they're outside my experience. She went to lots of different schools when she was a child (when dinosaurs walked the earth). Jan's father was in the army so they were always moving. Jan says I mustn't wait for people to come to me, I have to go to them, be pleasant and outgoing, be interested in them. I don't tell her that I've tried this already but still no one seems very friendly. Soph and Stace are OK, but they don't need me hanging around them all the time, I'm surplus to requirements. Perhaps I'll just have to do like Mr Hampton says and grasp the nettle of study – ouch!

CHAPTER THREE

When I wake up the house is really quiet. Dad and Jan got the Eurostar to Paris last night and I won't see them again until Monday after school. Freedom! I told Soph and Stace on Thursday that I'd have a parent-free zone this weekend and asked if they'd like to come round for pizzas and DVDs tonight. I was surprised how keen they were. I hope they'll agree to watch either *Face/Off* or maybe *Swordfish* and won't want to see something girly. Jan has a box set of *SATC* that her friend Sam gave her. It has a label on:

'For those times when you need to escape...Sam XX.'

I think I'll hide it to be on the safe side.

I spend the day giving the house a mega clean and tidy, which it badly needs. Jan can't see the point of dusting. She says someone called Quentin Crisp said it doesn't get any worse after the first four years. She told me he was a famous homosexual who came out of the closet before most people even admitted there was a closet, haha. She showed me a photo and I thought he looked a lot like my dad's sister Chris, only prettier. He's dead now, though not because he had a house full of dust. Jan gave me a book he'd written – *The Naked Civil Servant*. I might try it sometime – when I'm not grasping the nettle of study.

I decide to make some salad and some dips to have with the pizzas and chips. It might have been good to get takeout, but round here they think that's something you do with the bins.

I'm in the shower when the phone rings. It's Soph and she sounds really embarrassed. Apparently her mum has been talking to Stace's mum and they (the mothers) have decided that they don't want their precious little darlings mixing with the offspring of a murderer.

Of course she doesn't actually say that, but it's what she means.

I don't give her a hard time – it isn't her fault that she's the one who drew the short straw to tell me. I try to sound cool and say I think I'm getting bird flu or something so maybe it's better they don't come anyway.

'See you Monday, Emma,' Soph says. I can hear giggling in the background. I wonder if they'll even speak to me next week. I don't care.

I eat masses of pizza and watch some truly terrible reality TV. Dad and Jan would not approve. I'm hardly allowed to watch anything when they're around. After that I rummage through the DVDs and treat myself to *Grease*.

Jan phones to check up on me. I say the drug dealers and unsuitable boys have just left but will be returning later to wreck the house, haha. She doesn't think it's very funny. She and Dad are going somewhere on the Left Bank which is supposed to be this really cool part of Paris. I'd like to see it, but not with Jan and Dad. Jan would be pointing things out to me all the time instead of letting me look on my own and Dad would be holding my hand like I'm a toddler whenever we crossed the street.

I wonder if John's been to Paris. Then I remember he got married there. I watch another film – *A Civil Action*.

After that it seems like an excellent idea to practise my sax. At least here I don't have to worry about disturbing the neighbours. Back in Wandsworth, Dad used to say you couldn't even fart without someone at the end of the terrace hearing you. It's quarter to two when I finally head upstairs to bed.

*

Monday comes and I really do feel like I'm coming down with some sort of flu. But I force myself out of bed, make toast and coffee and eat an apple on the way to school. I can walk it in about forty minutes but sometimes I have a rare sighting of a rural bus going my way, which I take if I'm feeling tired or wet or both. I'm the wrong side of the tracks to be in Hillingbury High's catchment area and entitled to free school transport. The school I should go to is even further away though – and has a bad reputation. I wonder what it's like.

I get to school on time. Soph and Stace say 'hi' and smile but they turn away quickly. Oh well.

At assembly Mr Hampton says there's too much litter everywhere – do we want to live in a pigsty? Brainiac Bruce raises his hand and says it's never been demonstrated that pigs drop litter – science has yet to prove it.

Mr H thanks Bruce for his contribution and agrees with him. He says there are indeed times when the porcine character shows nobler qualities than that of the human being. He says he's decided to put Bruce's name at the very top of the new litter rota, which will apply to everyone in the school except the sixth form.

A brave little munchkin from Year 7 pipes up that he saw a Year 13 girl drop a fag packet and a Snickers wrapper just outside the gate. 'They're always dropping stuff, them lot.'

Other kids join in and say it isn't fair and why shouldn't the sixth form have to do it like everyone else? Mr Hampton roars for silence. He doesn't answer the question.

My new Word of the Week: porcine.

When I get home, Jan and Dad are slumped on the sofa.

'We've had a helluva journey,' Dad yawns. 'Make us a cup of tea, Em.'

They look like they've travelled halfway round the world instead of just across the Channel. Cigarettes are piled high by the bookcase.

Jan sees me looking. 'So much cheaper in Belgium,' she says. 'We did a detour on the way back.'

'I thought you were trying to quit.'

She sighs. 'Now is not the right time.'

The next morning Jan's up before me. She does this every now and again – gets an attack of domesticity. She's cooked enough carbs to keep an elephant happy for the day.

'Thanks,' I say, tucking into bacon, egg, sausage, beans, mushrooms, toast and – my favourite – tinned tomatoes with masses of black pepper. I love fried breakfasts.

'Good to see you enjoying it,' Jan says. She used to worry that I might be getting anorexic. It's true I didn't have much of an appetite for a while, around the time of Dad's court case. But anorexic? No way.

It's just as well I've had a big breakfast because something happens at lunch time that really makes me lose my appetite.

I'm about to tuck into my chicken salad sandwich. I'm at a table for eight but there's only me, Brainiac Bruce who's building something with Pringles instead of eating his pork pie, and a couple of small and silent Year 7 girls, both apparently deep in thought. I suppose we must look like the Sad Losers table.

Two girls come over. They're in my year but I haven't seen much of them before. They're not in my tutor group or any of my lessons except PE. One is tall with over-plucked eyebrows. The other's small, round and zit-ridden.

'Hi,' the tall one says to me. 'What's your name?'

Stupidly, I think she's being friendly, so I tell her.

'You're Katie – Cooper?' I say and, to the little one, 'Sorry, don't know your name.'

They sit down opposite me and the small one suddenly grabs Bruce's pie.

'I'm Megan Marsh. What do you think this pie's made of, Katie?'

'Well,' Katie says, 'if it's hers'– she jabs a finger at me – 'it must be human pie.'

'What?' I put down my sandwich. 'What did you just say?'

'Your dad's a murderer – we know,' Megan says. 'Killer's daughter – that's what you are.'

Bruce picks up his pie, wipes it on a piece of kitchen roll, and takes a bite. 'Actually the evidence of my taste buds suggests that this pie contains the finest organic pork,' he says.

'You shut your face, weirdo,' Megan growls at him.

'My father is not a murderer,' I say, trying to keep the wobble out of my voice. The Year 7 girls have stopped eating and are staring at us, transfixed.

'Killer's Daughter,' Megan says to Katie. 'That's what we'll call her, Killer's Daughter, Spawn of a Killer.'

'Your dad should be hung for what he did,' Katie says. 'My mother says they never should have abolished it. She says—'

But I never find out what else Katie's mother has to say because I jump up and grab Katie round her stupid throat.

'Shut up, you ignorant, stupid – porcine scumbag!' I'm yelling. 'You just shut up about my dad!'

'Miss, miss!' Megan's shouting. 'Help! Quick! Emma's trying to kill Katie!'

Katie punches me in the stomach and I kick her hard on her leg. She falls over and bursts into tears. 'That's my bad leg, you bitch.' She's rolling around and sobbing, turning up the

17

volume as – uh-oh – Mr Hampton comes striding towards us.

'Disgraceful,' he thunders. 'Utterly disgraceful!'

'Emma started it, sir,' Megan says. 'She just attacked poor Katie – she, well, she only asked if she could try some of her sandwich and Emma went ape, and—'

'Silence!' yells Mr Hampton.

'That's not true,' Bruce starts. 'The facts of the matter—'

'I said SILENCE, boy!'

'But—'

'Leave the hall.'

Bruce shrugs and glances at me. I try to smile, to thank him, as he pushes his chair in and heads for the door.

'Stop smirking, girl! This is no laughing matter. You'll come to my office after school today.'

I hang my head, there's no point in arguing.

'Ugly Killer's Daughter,' Katie whispers. 'You'll get yours now. I hope your killer father's worth it.'

I get the standard stuff from Hampton. He's studying my Permanent Record, frowning. I guess he's reading the bits about me being in fights before, at my last school.

'Why, Emma? You're a bright girl – exceptionally able in fact. Why blot your copybook by indulging in violent behaviour?'

'Other kids say things, sir. Sometimes I just have to hit them.'

'Sticks and stones, sticks and stones. If you feel you've been a victim of verbal abuse you must report it to your tutor. All the staff here have been trained to deal with bullying. We have a bullying policy in place, which has been used as a model in other schools. Each term we review strategies... what you must not do is to take the law into your own hands,

18

so to speak, and resort to savagery and blah-blah-blah-de-blah-blah.'

I look at the floor. I'm scared I might cry, so I say nothing.

'Do you wish to say anything?'

I shake my head. 'No.'

'Very well. Lunch time detention on Monday and Tuesday next week – understood?'

'Yes.'

'And if there is any more unacceptable behaviour we shall have to consider other measures.'

'Such as?'

'Such as, young lady, calling in your parents and sending you on an Anger Management course so you can learn to interact with others without resorting to brawling.'

When I get home Jan's in the kitchen, brandishing a wooden spoon, wiping her eyes on a piece of kitchen roll.

'What's up?' I say.

She's been crying, which isn't like her. I hope she and Dad haven't had a row or anything.

'Rats,' she says, bleakly.

I follow her slowly to the living room. I don't like rats either, but I'm not completely terrified of them as Jan is.

She shows me the uneven towers of cigarettes, obviously gnawed at the bottom. And there are droppings.

'Hell,' I say.

'It's a funny thing,' Jan says. 'They haven't touched your dad's.'

And it's true, they haven't.

'Perhaps they've escaped from a laboratory and they're addicted to your brand,' I say. 'Have they stolen your lighters too?'

We giggle.

'Do you think,' Jan says, 'you could possibly go to the village shop – see if they've got traps or something?'

'Can't you go? I've got homework.'

'I would, only I'm in the middle of making onion tartlets for tea. You can have some money for a Solero as well, if you'll go.'

'OK,' I sigh, in a long-suffering kind of way.

CHAPTER FOUR

The village shop is really strange. It stands on its own halfway down Spring Lane, about ten minutes walk from our house. There's parking for all of two cars alongside. In the window is a big hand-written notice in black felt-tip pen:

BROWN'S. FOR ALL YOUR EVERYDAY
REQUIREMENTS. WE HAVE AN UNRIVALLED
SELECTION OF BISCUITS. FRESH, FROZEN AND
CANNED GOODS OF ALL TYPES. WHY WASTE
FUEL TRAVELLING TO TOWN?

BECAUSE (I want to write underneath), THERE'S NOTHING HERE THAT ANYONE IN THEIR RIGHT MIND COULD POSSIBLY WANT OR AFFORD.

It's fitted out like a supermarket but there's no logic to it. So you get eggs at outrageous prices next to dusty candles; loo paper next to ketchup. 'Sell-By' and 'Best Before' are clearly alien concepts. There's a huge box of bargains ranging from faded black tights to bashed-up tins of butter beans. Radio Hayseed provides ambience.

I edge past the displays of misplaced apostrophes: special offer potato'es, organic cabbage's (twentieth century if I'm not mistaken) and tinned marrowfat peas' in brine. (Does anybody really eat that stuff?) And up towards the till. It really is up as the floor slopes.

Sometimes the owner, Mr Brown, is on duty, sometimes his wife takes a turn. Today it's Mr B. I've been in here four or five times but he still looks at me like I'm from Mars. He puts down his *Daily Mail* slowly and carefully, like he's scared it's going to fly out the shop if he doesn't keep watching it. I'm the

21

only customer, apart from Mrs Denny, who's deep among the unrivalled selection of biscuits.

'Excuse me,' I say, 'but do you have anything for rats?'

He sighs regretfully. 'There's no demand.'

'Any idea where...?'

'I don't keep pet food now – except Pedigree for the vicar.'

I sincerely hope the vicar has a dog.

'Didn't the pet shop supply you with any?' he asks.

'They aren't pets,' I say desperately. 'They're pests, vermin, wild rats – you know?'

Mrs Denny looks up sharply.

Mr Brown leaps to his feet. 'Wait here,' he commands, and disappears into the dark storeroom at the back of the shop.

He's gone for several minutes. I can hear a lot of banging and mutterings, during which time Mrs Denny approaches and stands directly behind me at the till, saying not a word. I can hear Mr Brown shout something and Mrs Brown shout something back. There's a loud crash and then he reappears, empty handed.

'I had some,' he said. 'Big traps – a bit rusty perhaps, but properly engineered, strong. And there was Warfarin.'

'Yes?' I don't much like the sound of this.

'Beryl had a clear out and gave them to the church jumble – stupid.' He shakes his head. 'Unbelievable.'

'Never mind,' I say. 'It doesn't matter.'

'You could try shooting them,' he yells, as I leave the shop. 'I've got shotgun cartridges.'

'We don't have a shotgun,' I say, trying not to laugh at the thought of Dad trying to hit a rat. He couldn't even win a coconut at my old school fair. And Jan and I would be equally useless.

'It's all quite legal,' Mr Brown insists. 'Are you sure you won't take some cartridges – in case?'

'No thanks,' I say.

I'm making a hasty exit when who should come waltzing through the shop door but Brainiac Bruce.

'Abandon hope, all ye who enter here,' I mutter to him.

'Eh?' He looks puzzled. Which is hardly surprising. Perhaps he's after some bargain bashed-up butter beans.

Jan's not too disappointed with my lack of success.

'Perhaps we'll get a cat – or two,' she says.

I'm so pleased I hug her. I worship and adore cats. Not the fat, fluffy flat-faced Persian types or the round, solid moggy types. Not Siamese, the noise is horrible and they're terribly bossy. My favourite cats live with my Grandma Persephone. They're small and graceful, beautiful with their pointy ears and pointy faces. There must be about ten of them; all the same family, Gran says – mostly ginger and white. They don't really have names but I gave them some the last time I was there. My favourite was Simba (after *The Lion King*). It just shows how long it is since I was in Kalos.

'Can we really have a cat?' I say to Jan.

She hesitates. 'I'll talk about it with your dad.'

She always calls him 'your dad'. Never by his name, Dino, short for Dionysus, who was the god of wine, vegetation and fruitfulness in Ancient Greece.

The following Friday, Jan and Dad decide to go to the next village for a pub meal. They ask me if I'd like to come but there's a John Travolta film I haven't seen for a while on TV – *Get Shorty* – so I decide to stay home. I'm just laughing at Danny DeVito when I hear a noise from the kitchen. I freeze. It's a sort a scrapey, scratchy noise and I've a good idea that it probably isn't the tooth fairy.

When the ad break comes, I creep into the kitchen to see. I can't believe it. There's a gigantic rat sitting on the draining board eating the pan scourer. It looks up at me, full of attitude. I have to get rid of it before Dad and Jan get back or Jan will have hysterics. I look round for a weapon. Not that I want to kill it, just frighten it away.

In the living room there's a pile of hardback books that were here when we came. I got really excited when I first saw them until I realised they were all Abridged Classics. They're now waiting for the next village jumble sale.

I pick up the books and take aim. *Great Expectations* follows *Lorna Doone*. The rat doesn't even blink. I try again and this time I get closer with *Daniel Deronda* and *The Mill on the Floss*. Then *Jane Eyre* knocks a glass onto the floor which unsettles the rat a bit, but not much. *The Tenant of Wildfell Hall* goes wide of the mark but *Hard Times* is more like it.

Finally *Sense and Sensibility* followed in quick succession by *Dombey and Son* and *Middlemarch* score almost direct hits. The rat decides it's had enough of bombardment by literature. It squeals horribly as it runs behind the back of the sink. Shaking slightly, I get myself a Coke and return to gaze once more at Mr Travolta.

Dad and Jan are quite late so I go to bed, hoping the rat's fast asleep somewhere. I read *Tess of the D'Urbevilles* for a while. I've got to do an essay on it over the weekend. I think I'll call it: 'Does Angel Clare Need a Good Slap?' Or perhaps I won't.

I hear Dad and Jan unlock the front door. Dad sees my light on and comes in.

'What's with all the books everywhere?' he asks.

I explain about the rat, whispering so Jan doesn't hear. 'Sorry,' I say. 'I forgot I hadn't picked them up again.'

Dad smiles and brushes his fingers against my cheek. 'Goodnight, Kyria Kitten.'

He hasn't called me that since I was about six years old. It's a bit babyish – but I don't tell him off.

'Night, Dino Dinosaur,' I say.

CHAPTER FIVE

When I get to school on Monday, someone (no prizes for guessing who) has pinned a poster-size, extremely crude drawing of me on the notice board outside the hall. Underneath it they've scrawled: EMMA ZENS – SLAG BOFF – KILLERS DAUGHTER.

There's one good thing about Hillingbury High – the Olympic-size indoor swimming pool. I just love to swim. There's a gala next week. I reckon I'm in with a good chance in the Under-16 Girls' Breaststroke and the Freestyle. My main rivals are:

1) Hayley Fletcher. She has an impressively athletic build; looks like she could swim the channel before breakfast and still do a day at school.
2) Stace. Though she tells me she hates the effect the water has on her hair (apparently the blonde isn't entirely natural), she still, like me, thinks swimming is ace. She's very good.

I'm sitting on the side after a practice race (I beat Stace by about three strokes) when Megan and Katie slither over. They sit down, one each side of me.

'You're not going to win at the gala, so you needn't bother thinking you are,' Megan says.

I decide there's no sensible answer to this.

'You're rubbish,' Kate says. 'We don't want rubbish in our swimming pool. Hayley will beat you, easy.'

'You think so?' I say thoughtfully. 'I reckon Stace's very strong – maybe she'll win.'

'Anyone's better than you, Killer's Daughter.' Megan rubs her hair dry.

'What about you?' I ask her. 'Think you've a chance of winning anything?'

'I don't care. Why should I care about a stupid gala? I don't want muscles. Boys don't like girls with muscles – don't you know anything, Killer Daughter?'

'I should think you've got a very good chance in the gala,' I say, giving her a good hard shove. 'You just need to practise...'

Megan lands back in the water and shrieks. Katie goes to push me but I'm too quick for her.

'You should do really well!' I shout at Megan. 'You look just like a fish – especially your face!'

'Megan Marsh, get out of the pool at once!' yells Miss Stone, the games teacher. 'Some of you girls – first I can't get you into the pool, then you won't come out!'

Megan splutters and swears – for which, I'm pleased to say, she gets a lunch time detention.

'Miss, miss, that's not fair. Emma pushed her in. It's all Emma's fault,' whines Katie.

'I wonder... Is Emma a ventriloquist, Katie?' Miss Stone asks.

'Eh? No. Dunno. What d'you mean?'

'Are you a ventriloquist, Emma?' Miss Stone turns to me.

'No, miss.'

'Then presumably you cannot be held responsible for the uncouth language coming from Megan just now?'

'Er, no, miss.'

'You see, Katie? It isn't Emma's fault. Megan is entirely responsible for her own foul mouth.'

I decide I rather like Miss Stone.

As Megan drips her way past she whispers to me, 'I'll get you for this.'

'I'm SO scared,' I whisper back. And I'm not. Well, only a bit.

Sticks and stones and all that. What can she possibly do to me?

I turn up for the first orchestra practice the following week. It isn't exactly the London Philharmonic. There are about twenty of us, mainly Year 7s and 8s. Violins and recorders rule. I'm surprised to see Brainiac Bruce there, changing the strings on an electric guitar. I hadn't thought of him as the guitar hero type. The guitar looks old and bashed about. He's the only person I vaguely know, so I go and say hi.

'I didn't know you played guitar,' I say.

He shrugs. 'Why would you? I didn't know you played saxophone.'

'Are they any good, this lot?'

'Not really.'

'Why do you come then?'

'Something to do. They might get better. I might get better. I don't get much chance to play at home.' He flicks his hair from his eyes, looking embarrassed.

The music teacher, Mr Brooks, comes in. My heart sinks – he looks about ninety-three. We sort ourselves out and then bash our way through a few standard tunes. Brainiac Bruce isn't bad, actually. I'm the only saxophone. Afterwards Mr Brooks comes up to me.

'Nice instrument you have there. Do you think you might moderate the volume a little next time? I fear the woodwind section will otherwise be inaudible.'

Judging by what I heard today, this would be no bad thing. But I smile sweetly and say I'll bear it in mind for next time.

'Perhaps you should sit with Bruce – our electric guitar maestro – in future.'

'Whatever. As long as that's cool with Bruce?'

Mr Brooks calls him over. 'Emma and I think it might aid the cause of musical harmony if you and she were to sit together.'

'All right,' he says, and to me, 'I thought you were a bit loud.'

'It's not that I'm loud,' I say. 'It's that everyone else is quiet.'

We have a Teacher Training day so I get up late. Jan is phoning the council's environmental health department about the rats. I wander through to Dad's workshop where he's sitting with a cup of coffee, smoking a cigarette and reading what looks like a magazine.

'Hi, Dino.'

He looks up quickly and smiles. 'Hi, Em. No school today?'

'Teachers are off. I did tell you . . . What you looking at?' I sit down at the workbench.

'Holiday brochure. An old one.'

'Are we going on holiday?'

He runs his hand through his hair. 'Don't think so. I'll have to earn some money first.'

'Have you done much recently?'

'No. A couple of pieces. Good thing we have no mortgage.'

I'm surprised he should say this. The money he inherited after Grandma Susie died was what made people suspicious in the first place.

'What about the website? I've said I'll help you.'

He looks exhausted. 'Thanks. Soon – we do it soon. If it won't interfere with your school work?'

'I can find the time if you can.'

As I leave the barn I glance at his brochure. It has a picture of blue sea and white houses on the front. Kalos – I knew it would be, of course.

*

'Could you go to the shop?' Jan says. 'We're desperately short of bread.'

'It'll probably be white sliced,' I say. I'm secretly pleased. I love white sliced but we hardly ever have it as Jan says there's no goodness in it.

Jan sighs. 'It'll have to do. I'm not driving miles just for bread.'

'How did you get on with the council?'

'They're sending a pest control operative.'

'Rat catcher?'

'Yeah. Can you get two loaves – and some bacon too? We could have bacon sandwiches for lunch.'

'Yum.'

When I arrive at the shop there's a new sign on the door. This one's written in red felt tip: CLOSED 4 LUNCH.

It's 11.30.

A strange woman is hopping up and down outside, glaring at her watch. She is tall and bony with a lot of frizzy grey hair escaping from what looks like a bootlace. She's parked her snazzy silver Mercedes badly, so that anything wider than, say, Kate Moss on a bicycle, will have difficulty squeezing past. But she has the hazard warning lights on, so I guess that's OK then.

'I say,' she brays at me, 'I say – do you know how long they shut for?'

'Um – about an hour, I think, usually.'

'Hell's Bellykins.' (I think that's what she says. You can tell she's not from around here and, call me crazy, I feel a sort of alliance with her just because of that.)

I'm about to go and come back later when she mutters something.

'I'm sorry?' I say.

'Pusskins are starving.'

'Are they? I'm sorry – what are pusskins?'

'Pusskins. My poor pusskins need their dins.'

I glance at the Merc and see, for the first time, two haughty-looking Siamese cats prowling up and down the parcel shelf. They're wearing red collars with imitation jewels (at least I assume they're imitation).

'Oh dear,' I say. 'What do they like to eat?'

She stares at me, almost as if seeing me for the first time, 'Whiskas, of course.'

'They don't stock it here – the man who owns the shop says there's no demand.'

'Bloody hell! Stupid man, of course there's a demand. Everyone needs Whiskas!'

I don't like to point out the obvious flaw in this statement.

'I say' – she puts a hand on my arm – 'you couldn't lend me some, could you?' Her fingers dig in.

'I'm afraid not,' I say, extricating myself.

'Oh please, please, pretty please.' She starts fumbling in her bag and produces a twenty-pound note. 'Just a few tins? I'll pay you twice the shop price.'

'I'm sorry,' I say. 'I can't lend you any, because I don't have any.'

'Why ever not?'

'Because,' I say helplessly, 'I don't have any cats.'

'No cats? No cats?'

'None,' I say, wondering whether to laugh or run.

'Then how the devil d'you know they don't keep Whiskas?'

'He told me – he told me in passing.'

At that moment Mr Brown's whiskery face appears behind the glass door. He seems startled to see two customers waiting. He undoes about a hundred locks and bolts and the shop is open once more.

We go to step inside as he holds the door for us. (Well, probably for Mercedes woman, I bet he wouldn't have held it if it had been just me.)

'One moment, please,' Mercedes woman says dramatically. She's effectively barring my way.

'Do you keep Whiskas?' she says slowly and carefully to Mr Brown, like he's maybe a foreigner or got learning difficulties.

'Certainly, madam, four varieties – tins and complete.'

'She, this girl, tried to tell me you didn't stock it.' She glares at me.

'But you said.' I turn to Mr Brown. 'Don't you remember? You told me there was no demand – except for the vicar's Pedigree?'

'You asked for rats, not cats!' He's outraged.

'Malicious,' says the woman, as she finally allows me inside. Cheeks burning, I make my way to the bread section where I encounter two so-called organic rolls that must be made of pure gold, judging by the price, and a petrified French stick.

'Hallo,' says a voice behind me. 'You're becoming a regular customer.'

I turn to see Brainiac Bruce.

'What are you after?' I say. 'Hope it's not bread, like me.'

'I'm not after anything,' he says. 'I live here – above the shop.'

I gaze at him. 'Is Mr Brown your dad?'

'Uncle. My dad's brother. Dad's dead.'

'What about your mother – is she Mrs Brown?'

(Why am I asking him these questions? He must think I'm demented.)

'God, no. My mother's started a new life in Crawley. Small flat – too small for my mother and the bloke and me, so I'm here with Uncle Hamish and Aunt Beryl – a.k.a. the Gruesome Twosome.'

We giggle. I want to say I'm sorry. People have such odd lives, you never know.

If you had asked me to guess about Bruce's family I'd have said: probably lives in one of those four-bed detached executive homes in Dairy Meadow with his brainiac father and his brainiac mother. No siblings; no pets unless reptilian; plenty of books but nowhere to put them; two medium range cars; holidays in Wales or the Lake District.

(Actually that's a lot of guessing. I had no idea until that moment that I'd speculated about Brainiac Bruce, however erroneously, quite as much as I had.)

'What did you want?' he asks.

'Sliced white bread – or any kind of bread really.'

'Walk this way.' He does this silly walk. So immature, and yet kind of funny. 'As one would expect, the sliced bread,' he says, 'lies adjacent to the dishwasher powder.'

I giggle. 'Thanks. Where's the bacon? Just tell me and I'll find it myself.'

'Wouldn't dream of it, madam,' he says, in a startlingly good imitation of his uncle. 'Please follow me.'

Our route takes us up near the till, where Mercedes woman is buying two crates of Whiskas. Mr Brown can scarcely conceal his delight. He's actually rubbing his hands.

'She must have lots of cats,' Bruce mutters.

'Siamese,' I say.

'How do you know? D'you know her?'

'Absolutely not . . . it's a long story.'

'That should do for now,' Mercedes woman's saying. 'Would you mind awfully carrying them to the car for me?'

'Certainly, madam.'

Bruce suddenly ducks out of sight. Not quite quickly enough.

'Bruce!' yells Mr Brown. 'Carry Out!'

'Damn,' Bruce whispers. 'Back in a minute.'

Mercedes woman catches sight of me once more. 'You can tell actually,' she says pityingly, 'that you wouldn't have cats.'

I can't think of a reply.

'It's people like me,' she says, 'who are responsible for this man's livelihood. Do you want to see the supermarket giants taking over the landscape?'

Actually a Tesco or an Asda nearer than a thousand miles away would be extremely useful, but I don't say this.

Bruce looks at us, mystified.

'Malicious,' says the woman again, as Bruce begins staggering towards the door with her cat food. And to Mr Brown she says, 'Thank you so much for your help. You will let me know when they bring out the smoked venison flavour?'

'Certainly, madam. I have your number.'

'Must fly. I have to get Romeo over to Lindsey's so he can serve her Petunia before she goes off the boil.'

Bruce nearly drops the boxes.

He comes back. 'Bacon this way.'

Mr Brown is looking at us, puzzled. We get to where the bacon should be, next to the disposable razors apparently, but there's none there.

'Come upstairs,' he whispers to me. 'There's about three pigs' worth in our fridge. You can borrow some.'

'Are you sure? I can do without.'

'Sure I'm sure. Just pay for the bread first.'

We pay for it, then Bruce says to his uncle, 'OK if I have a break?'

'And why did you not do so when we were closed?'

'Unpacking. Savoury snacks – assorted, remember?'

'Fifteen minutes then.' He takes my money, counting it carefully.

'I'm taking Emma upstairs,' Bruce says. 'She wants to borrow something.'

'Who's Emma?' says Mr Brown stupidly.

'Me,' I smile sweetly. 'I'm Emma.'

'Lord above,' says Mr Brown. 'The girl who's trying to ruin me.' But I think I can see a smile – or is it a snarl? – on his face. 'Fifteen minutes,' he yells, as Bruce and I climb the stairs at the back of the shop. 'No more.'

Bruce gives me two packets of back bacon from the impressively well-stocked fridge. Strangely, they've got Sainsbury's labels on them.

'Thanks,' I say, 'I'll replace them soon.'

'While you're up here,' Bruce says. 'Would you like to see my room?'

'OK.'

His room is big, nearly as big as mine but tidier. There's a sound system, a PC, a TV, nothing unusual – except...

Except that where there should be posters of the usual boy stuff – football heroes, rock stars, fast cars, fast girls – there are paintings. Beautiful Greek landscapes; people at a table; donkeys by an olive tree; sun setting over mountains.

'Who did these?' I say.

'The evidence points to me.'

'They are seriously good. Are you doing GCSE Art?'

'Nope. Uncle Hamish wanted me to do two languages, so I couldn't fit it in.'

'That's a shame.'

He shrugs. 'Don't care. Anyway, these aren't much.'

''Course they are.' I look at another of the landscapes. Tall green Cypress trees on a mountain above a flat blue sea. 'You've been to Greece? It is Greece, isn't it?'

'No and Yes.'

I think about this. 'Then how do you...?'

He laughs and pulls an old calendar from a drawer, turning the page to June. 'See? I just copy and add a few bits here and there.'

'Wow.' I look at the calendar: Scenes from Cephalonia.

'Never been there,' he says. 'Not likely to in the unforseeable future either.'

'I thought it might be Kalos,' I say. 'Same sea anyway. The Ionian.'

He looks at me carefully. 'Emma Xenos,' he says softly. 'Of course...'

'Of course what?'

'Your father...'

'What about him?'

'He was tried for that murder, wasn't he? That's what those two lamebrain girls were on about the other day at lunch.'

'YES!' I suddenly yell. 'And he was found Not Guilty – why doesn't anyone get that?'

'I guess it's because they never found the guy who did it. Look, I'm sorry. I didn't mean to upset you, Em.'

'Don't call me Em! You don't know me!'

I run down the stairs, grabbing my bread and bacon on the way.

Bruce doesn't try to follow me.

Malicious. That's my Word of the Week.

CHAPTER SIX

It's the day of the swimming gala. The steamy, chemical-smelling heat inside the building contrasts sharply with the chilly wind outside. Leaves crack against the windows. I've never liked Autumn. There's all that winter ahead, long months of it with hardly any sun. I shiver in the tropical changing rooms – nerves, that's all it is.

My first race is the Girls' Under-16 100-metre Freestyle. I think Hayley will ace it, but I stand a reasonable chance of second. Stace grins at me as we line up at the pool edge. The school is divided into four 'houses' named after sea creatures. Stace is a Dolphin, I'm a Whale, Hayley's a Seal. The other house is Stingray. There are eight girls in this race but I reckon we three are the main contenders.

We wait nervously for the starting pistol, which, anyone can see, Mr Hampton just adores. I'm sure that's why he's here today. He wouldn't normally be dragged away from his office for an intra-school competition – especially one with no parents present. But he gets to fire the gun, which looks like the kind of thing you see in old movies about World War Two. It makes the kids in Year 7 shriek every time he pulls the trigger and I notice some of the teachers flinching. It is seriously loud, especially in a building like this.

So we stand there, swaying slightly, toes balancing on the edge. 'Kerrrcacrack!' We're off and I'm swimming for all I'm worth but it's still not enough to catch Stace or Hayley as we come to the end of the first length. As we turn and I surface briefly I can hear all the kids screaming:

'See-yulls, See-yulls, Dol-phins, Dol-phins, Way-yulls, Way-yulls, Sting-ray, Sting-ray!'

I'm gaining on the winners, I really am. Stace is visibly tiring and Hayley's slowing down or I'm speeding up... Unbelievably, I touch the end first, with Hayley less than two seconds behind me. I look round for Stace but she must have got a stitch or something because an unknown Stingray is in third place.

I'm smiling so much as the victory cheers for 'Way-yulls' die down that I don't notice the judges (Mr Hampton, Miss Stone and a couple of LSAs) are in a huddle. Miss Stone approaches me.

'I'm sorry, Emma, disqualified I'm afraid.'

'What? Why?'

'Your tumble-turn at the end of length one was incorrect.'

I think for a moment. 'Are you sure? I thought I did it right.' Did I though?

She looks genuinely sorry. 'I'm afraid so.' She hesitates. 'Never mind – you should do well in the Breaststroke later.'

I nod, feeling sick and tearful and so angry with myself. I get out of the pool and make my way back to the changing rooms. The Under-16 Breaststroke isn't until after the lunch break. I pass Megan Marsh and associated witches on the way.

'Here comes the Killer Cheater,' says Katie. She thinks this is witty.

'Never mind, Emma,' Bruce says. 'Better luck this afternoon.'

We haven't spoken much since I stormed out of his bedroom. He's tried to talk to me but I've been avoiding him.

'Thanks, Bruce,' I say.

'She stands no chance this afternoon,' Megan says softly. 'No chance at all.'

After a possibly-too-huge portion of pasta and salad, it's soon time to return to the pool for the afternoon session. I'll be wearing my new electric-blue swimsuit – Jan treated me on Saturday. We're supposed to have at least two for the gala in case we catch pneumonia and die and our sorrowing parents sue the school. Stace only has one and is holding it under the hand drier so it won't feel too icky when she puts it on again.

'What happened this morning?' I say. 'I thought you'd get a podium position.'

'Stomach cramp – something I ate, I expect.'

'You notice how these things never happen at the right time – like at the beginning of Maths, say?'

She nods. 'Strange but true. I'm still feeling a bit yucky now – but I'll be all right.'

'Good luck anyhow.'

'Thanks – you too.' She turns away quickly. I tell myself this is because real athletes don't get too friendly with the enemy. But a moment later I notice her giggling with Hayley – feeling better, no doubt.

I get my bag down and feel inside for my swimsuit – and as I pull it out I go cold all over. Someone has cut it up the back – slashed the material. I hold up the tattered remains. It's completely useless.

'Emma!' Stace notices and comes over. 'What's happened?'

'The bitches,' I say hoarsely. I sit down heavily on the bench, wanting to cry, too angry to let myself do it.

'I'd lend you a spare – if I had one. Then at least you could do the race.'

I brighten up a bit. 'It's OK. I've got the one I wore this morning.'

But I haven't. We search the changing room; it's mysteriously vanished.

At last Stace stands on a bench and shouts: 'Someone's

destroyed Emma's new swimsuit and stolen her old one. Has anyone got a spare they could lend her?'

The silence is deafening.

'It's OK,' I say loudly. 'I didn't really want to compete anyway.'

I walk away.

Outside in the corridor I run across Bruce. For some reason I tell him what's happened.

'How long is it to your race?'

I check my watch. 'Fifty-one minutes.'

'In the words of the immortal Arnie: I'll be back.' And he's gone.

A glimmer of hope. Could it be that the village shop has swimsuits? Will they have been manufactured this century, or at least in the final decades of the last? I'm still mad as hell about my lovely new one, but at least there's a chance now I can still do the race.

Bruce arrives back with five minutes to spare. He hands me a small carrier bag.

'Thanks,' I say. 'You're a star.'

He looks embarrassed.

I run to the changing rooms and pull out the swimsuit. Stace is still in there, clutching her stomach.

'Wow,' she groans. 'That is seriously hideous!'

I nod in agreement. 'And the award for bad taste goes to ... I can't really wear this, can I?'

The swimsuit is about two sizes too big. It is purple, shiny purple, adorned with enormous orange cabbages and green triangles. When could it ever have been fashionable? It isn't new and I suppose, creepy thought this, it must belong to Bruce's Aunt Beryl.

'P'raps I'll say I'm wearing it for a bet.'

I wish I'd worn my hoodie or even a towel over my shoulders to hide the full blast of the swimsuit's repulsiveness, but, as it is, Stace and I have to run to our starting positions, meriting a hard stare from Miss Stone who's very hot on (not) running at the pool side. At least I think that's why she's staring. The crowd at the pool side fall silent as I pass. Then someone wolf-whistles, and the giggling echoes around the building. I'm beyond embarrassment now. I only want to win. I turn to look at Stace but she's staring straight ahead, focusing, waiting for the ear-splitting crack of the starting pistol.

I plough through the water, painfully aware that the ill-fitting swimsuit is slowing me down, concentrating on doing the perfect textbook turn at the end of the length. Stacey and I are together, Hayley's a couple of seconds in front. I sense, rather than see, that everyone else is light years behind. The turn goes perfectly, though Hayley is faster and surging ahead. The crowd screams and I'm scarcely aware of it. Stacey has dropped back behind me and suddenly I feel my left leg being tugged so hard, I'm almost dragged under. I half-turn, amazed and furious at such blatant cheating.

But as I look at Stace I realise she's in real trouble. Her face is grey and she's struggling to tread water. I'm no good at life saving, but somehow we avoid the others in the race and I get her to the side. Stace, who's practically unconscious, is hauled out of the pool, covered with a fleecy blanket and whisked away.

As I stand up, dizzy and defeated, the water pours out of the top of the swimsuit in yet another cringe-making moment.

Miss Stone approaches me. 'You OK, Emma?'

'Fine,' I say, shivering. 'Though I wouldn't mind some hot chocolate.'

'Get changed first, then come and find me.'

I feel slightly unreal as I find my way to Miss Stone. She asks the boy sitting next to her to make room for me on the bench and I squeeze into the gap.

'You did jolly well,' she says, handing me a polystyrene cup of chocolate.

'Thanks,' I say. 'How's Stace?'

She drops her voice. 'Off to hospital, possible peritonitis. D'you know what that is?'

'Yes. My father got it when his appendix burst a few years ago. Poor Stace.'

I take a sip of chocolate. Never has anything tasted so good.

'You didn't have to help Stacey,' Miss Stone says. 'We've got three lifeguards watching. She wouldn't have drowned, y'know.'

'I was closest.'

'But you might have won the race.'

'No chance. Hayley was getting away from me.'

Miss Stone thinks for a moment, then says, 'I expect Mr Hampton will want to see you – and your name will be read out in assembly.'

'What for? Having the world's ugliest swimsuit?'

Miss Stone laughs. 'It did look a bit – strange. Why did you wear it?'

I hesitate. 'For a bet,' I say. 'I wore it for a bet.'

The very next day I'm cornered near the bins by Megan Marsh, Katie Cooper and the two grinning mouth-breathers who sometimes hang around with them.

'We heard about your slashed swimsuit,' Megan says.

'Such a shame,' Katie says.

'That you weren't wearing it at the time.' Megan gives me a shove on my shoulder.

I stand my ground. The mouth-breathers snigger like it's the best joke they've heard in ages.

'I'll soon have proof who did it,' I say.

'How?' Megan sneers.

'I put special blue powder on it,' I lie. 'Like they do on banknotes? That stuff shows up on people's hands about twenty-four hours after they've committed a crime?'

Megan and Katie both glance quickly at their hands. Stupid. Not that I needed any proof really.

'Yeah, right,' sneers Megan. 'Like you could get hold of that stuff – Killer's Daughter.'

I smile steadily. 'You never know, Megan. I just might have contacts – you never know.'

I'm pleased to see they both look a teensy bit worried. Which is small consolation for how sick I feel inside at this moment.

'You looked really mingin' in that swimsuit,' Katie sneers.

'Mingin' dyke!' Megan contributes.

'Is that the best you can do?' I say. 'Pathetic.'

'You think you're so clever…' Megan spits.

I raise my hand, then tap the side of my head with my index finger.

'No, Megan, I know I am. Pity you can't say the same.'

I walk away quickly before they can come up with anything else. A stone hits the top of my left ear. It doesn't hurt much.

CHAPTER SEVEN

Stace has her operation and is expected back at school the following week. Her parents send me a bunch of flowers with a card saying 'With thanks from Max, Maria and Stacey Austin.'

Mr Hampton calls me to his office and, rather grudgingly, says 'well done'. To be fair, he's rather more generous when he gives me a mention. In assembly during the review of the swimming gala.

'Altruistic, quick-thinking, selfless,' he calls me.

Wow.

The effect is rather spoiled by someone calling out: 'Piss-poor fashion sense, though.'

Everyone laughs, even me. Mr Hampton demands that the culprit own up, but no one does of course.

He's got away with it, for once. I'll deck Bruce when I see him.

'I think,' Jan says, 'your dad and I might go to the Dordogne for a few weeks in the summer. Sam's invited us to stay at her holiday place.'

'Sounds good,' I say.

We're sitting eating toast in the rat-free kitchen on Sunday morning. Just the two of us. Dad's had a bad night and is catching a few more zeds.

'I don't suppose you'll want to come, will you?' Jan says. 'There's nothing much for teenagers there.'

'Of course not,' I say. 'I'm so used to a life of glamour and clubbing and shopping and hanging out with my friends – I couldn't possibly go anywhere like that. It'd be the pits.'

'There's no need to be sarcastic,' Jan says, pouring coffee. 'You can come if you like, naturally. I just thought it'd be too dull for you. There'll be two couples, besides me and your dad. I don't think they – the others – know about the court case and everything.'

'Don't count on that,' I say. 'Even if Sam can resist the gossip value.'

'Sam's my friend!' Jan is indignant, 'She wouldn't tell anyone if we didn't want her to.'

'Sorry,' I say. 'I'm sure you're right – it'll be OK. You'll have a great time.'

'My only worry is you,' Jan says.

'How d'you mean?'

'Well, if you don't come with us, what will you do?'

'I'll be fine,' I say.

The phone rings and Jan answers it. I can tell by the look on her face that it's another of the anonymous calls we've been getting recently. She slams down the receiver.

'That was another lunatic from the fan club – I think.' Her voice shakes.

'Probably kids,' I say, wishing I could believe it.

'That's what the police say.' Jan twists her shirt in her hands. 'I just wish they'd leave us alone.'

'Sticks and stones, sticks and stones.' I gulp at my coffee.

'What?'

'Nothing. It isn't important.'

CHAPTER EIGHT

Stace came back to school today. She still looks a bit pale.

'Thanks for the flowers,' I say, catching up with her.

'You're welcome.'

We scuff through the autumn leaves to our tutor room for morning registration. The wind lifts litter and drops it again.

'You OK now?'

'Fine – and thanks again for the rescue.'

Suddenly Soph comes running up behind us. This is quite impressive as she's wearing high-heeled boots and a tight skirt.

'Hi, you guys,' she says. And 'Welcome back, skiver,' to Stace, giving her a playful punch on the shoulder.

'Missed you too,' Stace says.

'You want to come Christmas shopping on Saturday? Dad's got to go to Bournemouth and he'll, like, give us a lift?' Soph asks her.

'Great, yeah. We can get chips from Harry Ramsden's, maybe?'

'What are you? Carbiverous now? We're going shopping, not to stuff our faces...'

Gradually they drift away and I'm left to walk alone. They didn't ask me. Probably not enough room in the car – except I happen to know Soph's dad has a big, blue, get-out-of-my-way-quick off-roader. Perhaps some other people are going... Perhaps they can't use that car because there's something wrong with it... Perhaps they just don't want me. Yep, that'll be it. Knew I'd get there in the end.

The end of term comes. Bruce gives me a seriously soppy Christmas card. On the front is a pink rabbit dressed as Santa;

46

inside the message reads: Have a Very Hoppy Christmas. He's signed it Bruce – no love or anything – thank goodness. I give him a card with a picture of snow-capped mountains. I sign it Emma.

I get through the Festive Season with Dad and Jan. We sit in front of the TV eating and drinking too much in a haze of tobacco smoke. I only eat too much. Dad and Jan try to persuade me to drink some wine but I don't much like the taste of alcohol. And I hate the idea of smoking (not that they want me to smoke). Sometimes I think I'm too much of a straight-edger.

I wish I had some excitement in my life.

For the next couple of months I grasp that nettle. Most of the teachers seem really pleased with my progress. I still have the occasional incident with Megan and Katie, but I do my best to keep out of their way. Once someone shoves me at the top of the stairs in the Arts Block, but I manage to grab on to the railing before plummeting to the ground floor.

Then there's the time when someone decides during PE that it would be a great idea to steal one of my shoes. I only discover its whereabouts when it blocks one of the loos, causing a minor flood. The caretaker – think Groundskeeper Willie in T*he Simpsons*, only less attractive – accuses me of doing it myself. I ask him why he thinks I'd want to deprive myself of half my footwear.

'You kids are just here to make my life hell,' he growls.

'Rats are back,' Dad says. 'I saw one run across the kitchen floor – don't tell Jan.'

Luckily Jan's away. Spending the weekend with her friend Sam in Wandsworth, or 'Up That London' as the locals say.

It's Friday. Dino and I are watching the early evening TV.

The local news is as thrilling as ever: man trips over paving stone and blames the council (yawn).

'What'll we do? About the rats? See if the pest control will come back?' I groan.

Dino sighs. 'Maybe. Maybe the village shop will have something in stock now?'

'Anything's possible.'

He gets up and zaps the TV. 'Let's go then,' he says.

I'm amazed – and a bit scared. Dino has hardly been out of the house since we moved here, and when he has it's usually been at night.

We enter the shop and luckily there's nobody there but Hamish behind the counter, reading *Exchange and Mart*. He looks up as we approach the till, scarcely glancing at me, scanning Dino carefully.

'Good-eve-ning-can-I-help-you?' he says. Apparently he thinks Dad can't speak English.

'I-don't-know,' Dino replies. 'We-have-a-rat-prob-lem. The-en-vi-ron-men-tal-health-de-part-ment-at-the-coun-cil-sent-the-pest-con-trol-bloke-but-the-rats-came-back-and-we-thought- you-might-have-some-poi-son. Or some other means of effective rodent extermination.'

I could kill Dad, though I'm having to try very hard not to laugh.

'Are you mocking me?' Hamish asks, eyes narrowing.

'Not even slightly. Are you mocking me?' Dino smiles one of his most charming smiles.

I can see Hamish is torn between wanting to make a sale and the desire to eject Dino from the premises. Luckily for us, avarice wins.

'Can you shoot?' he asks.

'Oh – yes,' Dino replies.

'Got a gun?'

'Er, no. Not just now.'

'If you buy the cartridges from me, I'll lend my gun to you – under supervision of course.'

This is unexpected.

'Well, I don't know…'

'I can come later on tonight, bring the gun, we'll do it together.' He looks at me. 'Maybe I'll bring my Bruce along.'

'Er – good,' I say.

'Shall we say eightish?' Hamish says.

'It'll be dark then.'

'Dark is good. I'll bring lanterns. And I know where I can lay my hands on a couple of Jack Russells.'

'Right. Fine. Thank you,' Dad says, faintly.

He buys his fags and we leave the shop. Once we're safely out of carshot I say, 'Serves you right.' And we both get an attack of the giggles.

'What's a bruce?' Dad says, when we've recovered.

'What d'you mean?'

'He said he might bring his bruce.'

This sets me off laughing again. 'It's a him, not a what, you dumb Greek. A true Englishman would-have-known-ex-act-ly-what-he-meant-by-that.'

CHAPTER NINE

At eight o'clock precisely, I open the door to Hamish, Bruce and two small terriers. The dogs immediately start yapping madly. They obviously consider that I'm invading their territory. Hamish bawls at them to shut up and they do so just as Dino comes downstairs.

'Would you like some coffee?' I smile at Bruce, who raises his eyes to the ceiling in a 'good grief' kind of way.

'No, no. Best get on.' Hamish unpacks a large holdall containing two guns, two lanterns, a quantity of cartridges, what looks like a packet of sandwiches, some dog biscuits and a transparent plastic bag wrapped around something slippery smelling of meat (very possibly liver).

We creep out of the kitchen door into the yard. Bruce and I have been assigned a dog each and the job of Rat Spotters. We take up our positions opposite each other, while Hamish and Dad stand side by side with guns at the ready. The pest control man had shown us the gap under the back steps where he thought the rats were getting in and had suggested cementing it over. Dino hadn't got around to doing that, so we stuff the opening with some old towels.

The dogs are getting restless, the lanterns are switched on – it's Showtime.

'Go,' Hamish says.

Bruce and I release the hysterical terriers who both dive off towards the shed and promptly disappear beneath it.

Suddenly they're coming. Three, four, six rats – more. I want to scream and run away but I'm rooted to the spot. Hamish and Dad start firing. The eyes of the rats shine yellow in the lantern light and their terrified squeaking

50

mingles with the delighted yapping of the dogs.

'Careful!' Hamish warns. 'Mind the dogs.'

I look at Dad. He's firing as fast as he can and – yes, he gets one. It seems to jump in the air as he hits it, then twitches and dies on its back.

'There's another one!' Bruce yells, and this time it's Hamish who ends the life of a rat. One of the dogs is shaking a large one so hard I think his head will fall off. Instead it's the rat's head that comes off. I turn and run back into the house, reaching the downstairs loo just in time to be sick.

Trembling, I swill mouthwash, then go to the kitchen to put the kettle on. I'm not going outside again, no way. And as I reach up to get the coffee I see it, cowering by the back door. It must be ill or it would have run somewhere. Rats are world champion finders of escape routes, the pest control man said. But this one is unmoving, regarding me with terrified eyes. It's small and grey, but the lower half of its body is large and distended. Perhaps it's pregnant. Even so, more so, it should have run. If I try to get past it to open the back door again, its life will end – death by dog bite.

I wonder what to do. I can't bring myself to go too close – so I look around for inspiration.

Perfect. There's a large cardboard tube that once contained some old maps of Kalos lying in the corner of the room. It's about nine centimetres in diameter. I pick it up and ease the red plastic caps off either end. Then I place one end as near the rat as I dare and, opening the window, I angle the tube to rest on the sill, the tube comes to an end about twenty centimetres after the window opening – looking good. I take a step towards the rat again, making faintly threatening noises, but it ignores me. Then without warning the back door opens and dogs and men appear together. This gives the rat all the encouragement it needs and it shoots off up the tube like there's no tomorrow, which of course there probably wouldn't have been if it hadn't shifted itself just then.

'What's going on here?' Hamish asks, as we watch the rat exit the tube and drop to the ground. 'Are you making pets of them again?' He shakes his head. 'It can't be done, you know. Even if you succeeded in taming them, they'll be full of disease.'

I can think of nothing to say, absolutely nothing. Dino is gazing at me as if wondering whether to save time by calling for the men in white coats right now.

Bruce is grinning. 'I wonder what its terminal velocity was,' he says.

'I'll give you terminal velocity, my lad,' Hamish says. 'Come on, get these dogs some water and biscuits.'

'Would you like coffee now?' Dino asks. 'Or something stronger?'

'Something stronger would be just fine.' Hamish grins as he goes through to the sitting room and makes himself at home. He sinks into the sofa, stretching his legs towards the log fire and wiggling his toes in their socks.

'I reckon we saw to most of 'em,' Hamish says. 'Fourteen's an excellent bag. I only got two more than that in the competition.'

'What competition?' Dino asks.

'Michael Dyer – hobby farmer near the river – he likes to hold one every year. The man with the biggest bag of rats by four o'clock wins a polypin of cider.'

Now that's what I call a quaint local custom.

Hamish gets out his cigarettes. 'You could enter next time,' he tells Dino. 'You're not a bad shot.' He says this rather grudgingly.

'Thanks,' Dino says. 'I haven't fired a gun for a few years, as you could probably tell.'

I look up sharply at this. I didn't know Dino had ever shot anything.

'We used to shoot birds,' he says to Hamish, 'when I was a boy in Greece.'

'That's horrible,' I say. 'How could you have done that?'

'How could I not have? Everyone did. It was tradition, a part of our lives.'

'Yuck.'

Dino's pouring two large whiskies.

'Coke?' I ask Bruce.

'Please.'

I fetch it for him. 'Shall we go to my room?'

Hamish and Dad are just getting comfortable. Dad's kicked off his shoes now and the terriers, no doubt exhausted by their work and the reward that followed it (Bruce fished two gigantic bones from the bag), are settling by the fire.

Bruce and I go upstairs with our Cokes and some Pringles. It's cold in my bedroom and I plug in the fan heater to warm it up a bit. He sits on my blue beanbag, I sit on my silver one.

Bruce looks around. 'No singers, no soap stars, no movie idols.'

'I like plain white walls.'

'What about if I gave you one of my pictures, for your birthday?' He looks away, suddenly embarrassed. 'You don't have to have one.'

'I'd love one; I'd really love one. Thanks, Bruce. But how do you know when my birthday is?'

'I looked on the register. June 15th – right?'

'Right. When's yours?'

'That'd be telling. You'll have to conduct your own research if you want to know.'

'You mean, look at the register, like you did?'

'Er, that would do it, I suppose.'

We smile at each other.

'I'll put on some music.'

'You don't have to. I'm quite happy just eating these and talking.'

'OK,' I say. 'Probably a good choice. I don't have that many CDs.'

'What do you like?'

'Jazz saxophone. How about you?'

'Metallica, Marilyn Manson, Nine Inch Nails, Nick Cave, Tom Waits – loads of people really.'

'*Chacun à son goût.*'

'What?'

'French. It means each to his own taste.'

'I knew that.'

'Oh, yeah.'

We throw Pringles at each other for a bit, then out of the blue he says:

'Emma – would you go out with me?'

'No!' I say, a little too emphatically.

He looks like I've just slapped him across the face.

'But I'd really like us to be friends,' I say quickly.

'Well,' he says, recovering, 'that's what I meant, really.'

'Don't take it personally.' (Like he can take it any other way.) 'It's just that – I don't want to go out with anyone – except maybe John Travolta.'

'He's ancient.'

'*Chacun à son goût.* You want another Coke?'

He sighs. 'If I know Hamish, we'll be here for a while yet. So yes, please.'

'Who would you go out with? If you could go out with

someone famous?'

'Never thought about it really. I mean, it's never going to happen so why bother?'

'Dreams. Suppose you were on a boat full of celebs and there was a shipwreck – who would you choose to get washed ashore with?'

'You're weird, Emma.'

'I know. It's a gift.'

He smiles. 'I think I like weird.'

It's just before midnight when Hamish shouts up the stairs to say he's going. Bruce and I have talked lots and watched half a video, *Phenomenon*, which Bruce hadn't seen before.

'You can borrow it if you like,' I say. 'See how it ends.'

He hesitates. 'I'd rather watch it with you again sometime, if that's OK?'

'Of course.'

I'm surprised when he kisses me on the cheek.

'Friends,' I say.

'Friends,' he smiles.

'Bruce!' Hamish yells. 'Get yourself down here, NOW!'

'Did you have a good time last night?' I pass Dino his coffee and some painkillers fizzing in a small tumbler of water. 'You don't look so good.'

'Thanks. I don't feel so good.' He gazes around the living room, shielding his eyes from the weak sunshine that's struggling to get through the grubby window. 'Got to clear up a bit, before Jan gets back.'

'We will. She won't be back before sixish.'

'Do you think he knew?' Dino says abruptly.

'Who, what?'

'Mr Brown – Hamish – about me and the . . . court case.'

I consider this. 'Probably. Aren't village shops supposed to be warehouses for gossip? And Bruce knows; well, he knows some, anyway.'

He looks up sharply. 'What did he say?'

'Nothing. I – I told him I didn't want to talk about it.'

'Is Bruce your boyfriend?'

'Dad!'

'OK. I mind my own business.'

'You should say I'll, not I. I'll mind my own business. And Bruce is just a friend.'

'Just you remember,' he says, 'I speak much better English than you speak Greek.'

'Whose fault is that? I'm not allowed to go to Kalos again now, am I?'

Perhaps I'm shouting, I do sometimes, almost without noticing – Loudmouth Syndrome, Jan calls it.

'Don't give me hard time.' He puts his head in his hands. 'Not my fault – remember?'

Strange how his English deteriorates when he's tired or stressed.

As we're eating supper with Jan later that evening she drops it on me.

'Sam wants us to go in May, to the Dordogne, before the crowds arrive.'

'That's really soon.'

'I know.'

'How long for?' I spear a potato.

'About four weeks.'

I put down my fork. 'It was three before.'

'I know.' She says it again. 'The thing is, Em, she wants us to look at some houses while we're there.'

'Why? Is she going to buy another one?'

She looks at Dino, Dino looks at her. He finishes his mouthful.

'We're thinking of moving there,' he says at last.

'But we've only just moved here!'

'I know, Kyria. But this, here, it isn't working...'

'What do you mean? We've only been here a few months.'

'Are you happy? Am I happy? Is Jan happy?'

'I'm OK. It's not that bad...I'm, I'm just getting used to things.'

'And what about the bullying?'

'What bullying?'

'You're saying there is none?' Jan cuts in. 'Your swimsuit didn't slash itself now, did it?'

I stand up and push back my chair. 'You can't make me move! I don't want to live in bloody France! What about my GCSEs?'

'You're a bright girl, Emma,' Jan says. 'We could easily sort something out about your education.'

I storm off toward the door, despite the fact that I'm still hungry. As I reach it, I turn to them. 'And what about this little trip in May? What am I supposed to do then? You needn't bloody think I'm coming with you to stinking France on holiday!'

That look between them again. They've obviously got everything planned.

'We thought,' Jan says, 'that your Aunty Chris might like to come and stay, keep an eye on things. At least for a couple of weeks. Don't forget you've a week's half term in May. You could come out to France then – have a look around the area...'

'You have to be joking!' I slam the door on my way upstairs.

57

They can't do this to me. I stamp about a bit. Then I decide I'll go and see Bruce.

I wish I had a mobile like everyone else. Dino says they give you cancer. I tell him so do cigarettes. He says his lungs are mature and my brain is immature. (Gee thanks, Daddy dear.) He says I can irradiate my head all I want when I'm eighteen. Jan says I should have one (a phone, not a brain) like everyone else.

I'm not like everyone else and this is just another example of that fact.

I bang on the back door of the shop but no one replies, so I go round the front. After a while the window above is opened and Hamish peers out.

'We're closed,' he says. 'Open again at 8.30 sharp tomorrow morning.'

'It's me, Mr Brown – Emma. Is Bruce in?'

'I said we're closed.'

'But I—' He shuts the window and I'm left looking up at it. Oh well.

When I leave for school on Monday morning, Dad and Jan are still asleep – dreaming about the bloody Dordogne, no doubt. But as I walk off down the road, Jan calls me back.

'Can you get us one or two things after school?' She yawns, shoving a list and some notes into my hand.

I don't even bother to ask her what's stopping her doing her own shopping. Too busy making 'to do' lists for France, no doubt.

I look for Bruce but there's no sign of him. I say hello to Stace and Soph, but they obviously don't hear me, because they walk right on by without stopping. I'd be paranoid to think that they had noticed and were ignoring me.

The first lesson's English. We're having a break from Gloomypants Hardy and are reading through a play called *The Crucible*. It's about witchcraft and false accusations and is a metaphor for America in the 1950s, Miss Tidesman says.

'Have any of you ever been unjustly accused of something? Or can you think of anyone else who's been in that situation?'

No one raises a hand. Some are gazing out the window, some are doodling.

'Anyone?'

Why is she looking at me? I look away and decide now is the ideal time to sharpen a pencil or two. Miss Tidesman sighs. Resigned to the fact it's Monday morning.

I've been summoned to see Mr Hampton – what am I supposed to have done now?

He asks me to sit down, then starts. 'I've had a complaint,' he says, 'and I'd like your comments.'

'What is it?' I try to look interested, concerned and intelligent all at the same time. I expect I'm scowling.

'Someone,' he says, 'has seen fit to place a quantity of cat excrement into Megan Marsh's backpack.'

'How do you know it's cat?' I say, interested. 'Did someone see it happen?'

'I – er – don't know how they knew its provenance. What I wish to know is, did you have anything to do with this?'

'No way! Why should I? I don't even have a cat!'

'I hardly think that ownership of a feline animal is a necessary prerequisite for the execution of this filthy deed.'

I ignore this. 'Why do you think I'd do it?' I say, feeling my face get hot. 'I don't do stuff like that!'

He shifts in his chair. 'It is well known that the two of you are not on good terms. Both of you have something of a reputation, behaviour-wise. However I have to say that, with the odd exception, I have no cause to complain about your conduct of late. I think being at Hillingbury has matured you – wouldn't you agree?'

I shrug my shoulders. 'Maybe.'

'However,' Mr Hampton continues, 'someone is responsible for this . . . befoulment.'

Befoulment? Is there such a word? If there is I'll definitely make it my Word of the Week.

Hampton's looking at me keenly.

'Well, it isn't me! I wouldn't touch her backpack and I don't play with shit, cat or otherwise.'

'Language, Emma, language. I'll overlook it this time. Normally it would, as you know, mean a detention. You'd better get back to your classroom – if you're quite sure you can't help me.'

I slam his door as loudly as I dare.

CHAPTER TEN

Bruce arrives in the lunch hour. It's a strange thing but we often don't talk much to each other at school. I guess neither of us wants people to think we're going out together, which is automatically assumed if you speak more than three consecutive sentences to a boy.

Anyway, I go over to Bruce, who's looking a bit furtive.

'Hi, where've you been?'

He mumbles something.

'What? Pardon?'

He sighs, then gives me a huge grin. Blue train-track braces run across his teeth.

'Cool,' I say. 'Did Hamish tell you I called last night?'

We walk across to the trees near the tennis court and sit on a bench, not too close to each other.

'Yeah, he told me. He also said I wasn't to associate with you any longer.'

I'm stunned. 'Why?' I say in a small voice. I can feel tears welling up, dammit. I am not going to cry. I won't let myself.

'Because of your father – what he did.'

'Firstly,' I say, trying to keep the wobble from my voice, 'my father, as I'm so sick of saying, was found Not Guilty.'

Bruce looks embarrassed. He appears fascinated by the leaf next to his foot, staring at it fixedly.

'And why?' I continue. 'Why has Hamish decided this now? We've been – friends – for ages.'

'He only just found out. Well, that's not quite right. He knew there was a – suspected murderer – in the village, but he thought it was some Cypriot guy who'd moved up Dairy Meadow – you know the new houses? He was seriously frosty

61

to him whenever he came in the shop. I used to wonder what that was about. But then, he's often weird with the customers.'

'So when did he realise? How did he?'

'I think he began to wonder the other night, after the Rats. He questioned me, but I pretended I didn't know what he was on about. It was Mrs Denny – your neighbour – she put him right. I guess the guy from Dairy Meadow's going to be amazed by the change in service next time he comes in.'

I almost laugh. It would be funny if it wasn't so awful.

'Are you going to orchestra practice after school?' he says, changing the subject.

'Yeah, probably. Are you? Or aren't you allowed because I'll be there? I'll give it up if you like – make it easy for you.'

'Emma, I . . .'

Suddenly my head's jerked backwards.

'Get up, Killer's Daughter.'

Megan Marsh has come from behind and got me by the hair.

'Ow! Let go!' I struggle to my feet, try to free myself, but now she's got my arm twisted behind my back.

Bruce jumps up. 'Leave her alone.'

'Ooooh, leave her alone,' Katie mimics him. 'You keep out of it, Metal Mouth.'

The mouth-breathers snigger stupidly; there's four of them plus Megan and Katie.

I struggle and kick out, but I can't connect.

'Do it,' Megan commands. 'Stick it in her hair.'

'Don't,' Bruce says.

Katie gives him a shove and he overbalances, hitting his head on the bench. For one horrible moment, I think they're going to plaster me with cat crap. Then they all open their mouths and take out chewing gum.

62

They stick it in my hair while I struggle and yell. Is everyone deaf as well as blind round here? Can't they see what's happening? Bruce is trying to grab their arms but it's too late.

'Now spit,' Megan commands. And they do, several times. They have surprisingly good aim.

'And kick.'

Like Daleks, they obey.

'That'll teach you to crap up my bag, Killer's Daughter,' Megan says calmly. Then she slaps me across the face, hard. Her ring with its pink 'diamonds' scratches my cheek. The no-jewellery rule doesn't seem to apply to Megan.

'Let her go now,' she says.

One of them has been standing back, filming it on her phone.

'I didn't touch your bag,' I say through clenched teeth. 'But I really wish I had, you piece of shit.'

That's it then. She hits me again, I hit her, and the next minute we're rolling on the ground. I get in a fair few punches and a good clump of her greasy hair comes away in my hand. In seconds, it seems, there's an audience around us, urging us on. More phones are produced to capture the action.

'FIGHT! FIGHT! FIGHT!' they scream in delight. It's over much too soon. Teachers come running, we're pulled to our feet and shouted at, marched off to see Mr Hampton. As we go, I see Bruce standing in the disappointed crowd; he looks stricken.

'It seems to me,' Hampton says, 'that this disgraceful business is basically six of one and half a dozen of the other.'

Megan and I are sitting on chairs opposite him. He glares at us from behind his desk. At least they let me wash my face before escorting me up here. I couldn't stand their loathsome spit on my skin a moment longer.

The chewing gum in my hair will have to be sorted later.

'What she done to me was way worse than what I done to her,' Megan scowls. 'She was well out of order. I had to get a new bag and most of my books went straight in the bin.'

'I didn't touch your bag,' I say. 'You attacked me, stuck my hair with chewing gum, spat on me, kicked me.' I turn to Hampton. 'How exactly is that six of one and half a dozen of the other, sir?'

'Don't take that tone with me, Emma,' he says. 'You, young lady, are on very thin ice.'

'And you're a liar. Someone saw you doing it,' Megan snarls.

Hampton looks interested at this. 'You didn't mention this before, Megan. Who was it who witnessed the bag incident?'

'No one could have seen me do anything,' I say, 'because I didn't do it. Why can't you get that through your thick skull?'

'Katie saw her!' Megan says, desperately. 'She'll tell you.'

'Katie'd say anything you asked her to. How very convenient that she's the supposed witness.'

'We'll come to that later,' Hampton interrupts. 'You don't deny that you were both responsible for the playground brawl just now?'

'She started it,' Megan said. 'Calling me names.'

'Did you start it?' Hampton says.

'I—' Suddenly I just want out of there. I can't take any more. I stand up to go. 'I'm leaving,' I tell Hampton. 'Enough's enough.'

'Sit down, Emma,' Hampton says angrily, 'we haven't finished yet.'

'I have,' I say. 'You can do what you like.'

'That's right, run away – just like your killer father,' Megan sneers.

I slap her hard across the face, then push the chair over so

64

she bangs her head on the floor. 'I hope that really, really hurts!' I yell. Then I run.

I run out of the school gates and away up the road towards the river. The wind's in my face and I feel free. I am never, ever, going back to that place. I wish I had my jacket though. I'm torn between wanting to throw my horrible blazer in the hedge and being grateful that at least it's giving me some warmth and protection from the cold drizzle that's started up.

I definitely don't want to go home. I feel in my pockets and discover, oh joy, that I've got thirty quid in my purse – for the things Jan wanted me to get on my way home. As if in answer to my prayers, the town bus comes along and I jump on, hoping the driver doesn't notice my disgusting hair.

'School's out early today,' she says pleasantly as she gives me my change.

'Dentist,' I mumble.

As we roll along the country lanes I start to feel a bit calmer. The bus is warm and surprisingly comfortable, though it smells a bit of wee and cheap sweets. There's no one on it yet but me and a couple of pensioners chatting to each other. I suppose Hampton will finally have the excuse he's been looking for to slap a permanent exclusion on me now. Not that I want to go anywhere near that poxy school ever again.

In town I treat myself to a Mars Bar and a smoothie, hoping one will cancel out the other. I pass a hairdresser with an 'Appointments Not Always Necessary' sign.

Forty minutes later and twenty-two pounds poorer, I have new hair. Very short, very now. The hairdresser swallowed my story about a pesky little brother playing a trick on me with chewing gum.

'I expect your mum gave him what for,' she says, smiling.

I smile back, feeling suddenly very tired. By the time I get back to the village, I have precisely three pounds and forty-two pence left of Jan's money.

I trail into the house and, of course, they pounce on me immediately.

'Where the hell have you been?'

'What's happened to your hair?'

'We've been worried sick!'

'We've got to see your headmaster tomorrow!'

'What's happened to your hair?'

'You might be expelled, or excluded, or whatever it is they call it!'

'We had no idea!'

'What's happened to your hair?'

'How could you?'

'Why did you?'

'What's happened to your hair?'

'We were on the verge of calling the police!'

'What's happened to your hair?'

And on and on and on and on. I don't say much beyond the bare essentials until Jan says, 'I think you've been really immature and selfish, Emma!'

Then I snap. 'What about you? How do you think I feel? You're going off to France and it's quite obvious that, as usual, I'm just going to be a nuisance. One more "problem" for you to work through. I'm telling you now, the two of you can run away abroad if you want – but you needn't think I'm coming with you!'

'Please don't shout at Jan,' Dad says, quietly.

'It's OK for her – and you – to shout at me, though, is it?'

'Don't get off the spike. Are you really saying you don't want to move to France?' Dad looks genuinely puzzled. How can he be so dense?

'Well, DURR. That's right.'

'Nothing's been decided yet,' Jan says quickly. 'And don't talk to your dad like that. He's only trying to help you.'

It goes on like this for a bit. Then we stop and have a meal, more or less in silence.

It seems to me what's really bugging Dad and Jan at the moment is the nuisance of having to accompany me to see Hampton tomorrow. I will definitely not be going. They can do what they like.

CHAPTER ELEVEN

After supper I ask if I can go for a walk, though I'm dead tired. They don't seem to mind; still stunned by this afternoon I expect. Before I leave the house, I phone the village shop. Luck's on my side: Bruce answers.

'Can you meet me?' I say.

There's a bit of a pause. 'I don't know. When?'

'Ten minutes. By the bus stop?'

'I don't think I can, Emma.'

In the background I hear the sound of the till.

'Are you in the shop?'

'I'm serving a customer right now.'

'So you won't come then? Fine.'

I slam the phone down and leave the house.

I find myself walking towards the bus stop anyway. I can't face being at home and there doesn't seem like anywhere else to go. In the distance I see someone approaching. It's Bruce.

'Thought you weren't coming,' I say.

'It wasn't easy.' He's a bit out of breath. 'Hamish wasn't pleased. I told him I had to see someone urgently about homework. Luckily that mad cat woman came in and he was so busy kiss-arsing her I managed to escape.' He looks at me. 'Cool hair.'

'Thanks,' I say. 'It's a bit cold round the ears but I expect I'll get used to it, and my head feels much lighter. Shall we walk in the woods?'

'So,' Bruce says, as we make our way along the path, weaving through the tall trees, 'what's up?'

I tell him all about France, about my interview with Hampton, about bunking off. (He knows about that. Apparently the whole school knows about that.)

'Anyway,' I say, 'I guess I just wanted to say goodbye, mainly. And it's been fun.'

'What do you mean? I thought you said just now you weren't going to France.'

'I'm not. But I won't be at school any more. And don't you remember this afternoon? You told me Hamish said you can't see me.'

He doesn't say anything. We've stopped in a clearing. The sun is doing its best to send a few rays down through the green before nightfall.

'It's OK, y'know. I do understand,' I say. 'It was bound to happen sooner or later I guess.'

'Bullshit,' he says. 'If you think I'm giving up being friends with you just 'cos Hamish doesn't approve, you aren't nearly as smart as I thought you were, Emma.'

Then, amazingly, his arms are round me. He's pulling me close to him and kissing me hard on the lips.

My arms go round him. I'm kissing him back. Suddenly he jumps back.

'Ouch!'

'What's wrong?'

'Bloody brace,' he says. 'The orthodontist told me to be careful kissing my girlfriend. Funny thing, this morning, I thought it was advice I didn't need.'

'Hilarious,' I say. We walk back to the road together, holding hands.

Chapter Twelve

Next morning we go to see Hampton. He sees Dad and Jan first, then asks me to join them. The upshot is, he suspends me for a week and agrees to give me one more chance to get my act together. I think he would have liked me gone for good, but I guess Jan can be quite articulate and persuasive when she wants to be. I also can't help wondering if my grades may have influenced him – Hillingbury's place in the GCSE league tables can only be helped by a brilliant student like wot I am. Little does Hampton know I might be gone before the end of Year 11 anyway, if Dino and Jan get their way.

I bet they didn't mention their plans to live abroad – not that I'll be going with them, whatever happens. As we're leaving Hampton's office I see Megan Marsh sitting with a large, determined-looking woman, whom I'm guessing must be her mother. I'm surprised to see Dino giving Megan a real chiller of a stare. She looks away, biting her fingernails.

Hampton looks a bit sick when he sees Mother and Daughter Marsh.

Once Dino's passed her, Megan gives me the finger. I ignore her.

On the way out of school I collect my saxophone from the music room. It's not in its case and someone (guess who?) has scratched the c word inside the horn. It'll probably polish off. I manage to hide it from Dino.

The week off is boring, but I get loads of work done and even find time to practise my playing. I can't see Bruce, but we talk a couple of times on the phone.

I try to get Dino interested in the business website I think he should have, but he just looks at me in a sad sort of way. I suppose I'm another of life's disappointments, as far as he's concerned. He tells me I'm my own worst enemy, which I think, as dumb remarks go, ranks up there with the best.

It's the last day of my suspension from school. We're eating a rather dubious-looking homemade soup that Jan's concocted.

'By the way,' she says, 'you'll be pleased to know we aren't going to the Dordogne next month...But the bad news, as far as you're concerned, is that we will be going in the school summer holidays.'

I tear off some bread. 'Does that mean me, too?'

They exchange a look. 'Of course you'd be welcome to come with us,' Jan says, 'but as you weren't exactly enthusiastic last time, we sort of assumed you wouldn't want to.'

'You got that right.'

Jan frowns. 'We'll be gone for four weeks, so you can't stay here alone all that time.'

'Don't see why not. I'll be sixteen by then, for God's sake.'

'Anyway,' Dad cuts in, 'you'd be lonely, all by yourself here.'

'No, I—'

'SO,' Jan interrupts loudly, 'we've arranged for you to stay with your Aunt Chris for three of the four weeks.'

'You mean she's coming here?'

That look again. 'No, Emma. She can't leave the dogs, she says. She wants you to go stay with her ...'

'NO WAY!'

71

'Yes way. Please don't shout. It might do you good to have a change of scene. And you can come out to France for the last week.'

I push my chair back and leave the room. I'm nearly crying. What next? What will they do to me next?

That night I watch *Look Who's Talking* to try to cheer myself up. It doesn't work.

CHAPTER THIRTEEN

'What's she like then, your aunt?' Bruce says.

We've taken to meeting up in the school library every lunch time. I didn't tell him about the summer holidays at first, hoping Dad and Jan would change their minds; but they won't. I thought Bruce might be hoping we could spend more time together once school was out. I know I was.

'What's she like?' he says again.

'Gruesome. Old. Fussy. Hates everyone. Breeds Pekinese. Smelly. Probably clinically insane.'

'Bummer. When are you supposed to be going?'

'Right after we break up.' I kick the table. 'I can't bear to think about it.'

Bruce sighs. 'I have bad news too.'

'What?' I feel the urge to hold his hand, but Miss Read (good name for a librarian) is watching us with her usual glassy stare.

'My mother,' Bruce sighs, 'has had a sudden attack of maternal instinct. She wants me to spend the summer holidays with her.'

I look at him, horrified. 'But that's terrible. How much of the summer holidays?'

He shrugs. 'Dunno. A few weeks I guess. Hamish isn't best pleased. The shop usually gets quite busy with tourists and weekenders.'

'Where did you say your mother lived?'

'Crawley. In a flat. With her boyfriend. I just know it'll be the pits, Emma. She'll get bored with me after a couple of days, but she won't want to lose face with Hamish so she'll insist I stay.'

'It's so unfair, isn't it? We're just pushed around for their convenience.'

'Maybe we don't have to be, Em...I've been thinking—'

'What?'

'Can't say yet – I'll tell you when I've thunk a bit more.'

Then it's the weekend and Bruce and I have managed to meet up in Salisbury. Bruce is supposed to be working on stuff for Project Neptune (which is this award thing we have to do at school involving personal challenge, community work, etc). I'm supposed to be looking out for something for my birthday that Dad and Jan can buy me. Jan and Dad wouldn't mind me seeing Bruce, probably. But somehow I want to keep our relationship to myself.

We're eating chicken tikka sandwiches on the grass in the Cathedral Close. It's nice here. Tourists wander about and the cathedral clock bongs impressively. I'm admiring a sculpture of a walking woman, wishing I could just walk away from my life: 'feeling sorry for myself', as Jan puts it. Bruce is sitting down, back propped up against a tree.

'You know what the problem is,' he says, as I join him.

'Nope.'

'The problem is, that no one believes about your father being innocent.'

I blink. 'Tell me something I don't know.'

'Emma?'

'That's my name.'

'Do you trust me?'

I look into his eyes. I've never noticed before how very dark brown they are. Almost black. It's hard to see where the pupil ends and the iris begins.

'Well?' he says impatiently.

I lean over and kiss him lightly on the mouth. 'One hundred

per cent,' I say. 'Why are you asking me?'

He takes a deep breath. 'Because I think you should tell me what really happened. How your father got into the – situation.'

'Why do you want to know?' I twist grass between my fingers.

'Because,' he says, 'I think it might help you to tell me. I know something about it – I read some stuff on t'internet . . .'

'Why? Why did you do that? When did you?'

'Because I was interested in you I suppose.'

'Trying to decide whether I really was a killer's daughter before you made up your mind to like me.' I'm tearing up the grass in handfuls now.

His face reddens. 'I thought you knew me better than that.'

We glare at each other. A large man approaches us, clutching a guidebook.

'Excuse me,' he says. His accent sounds German. 'Can you direct me to Stonner Honger?'

'Er, I'm sorry,' I say. 'I'm afraid I don't know it.'

'Is it a place in town – or a village?' Bruce asks.

'But you must know it,' the man expostulates. 'You must!' He thrusts the book under my nose. 'See here. Stonner Honger!'

'Stonehenge!' Bruce and I chorus, then start to giggle.

'Yes!' the man says angrily. 'That's what I said – Stonner Honger!'

This produces fresh merriment. The man walks off in disgust.

'Sorry,' Bruce calls after him. 'Sorry.'

The giggles have broken the glaring spell. I sit closer to Bruce.

'It's a long story,' I say. 'You'll have to buy me an ice cream when I've finished telling it.'

75

'You'll have to buy me one for listening,' he retorts.

He laces all his fingers through mine and pushes me over backwards onto the grass. He kisses me. I'm getting to like it.

'No kissing, by order of the Dean and Chapter,' I say, sitting up, brushing the grass from my jeans.

'Spoilsports.'

'Do you want to hear this story?'

He sits up, runs his hands through his hair. 'Yes, I do.' He's suddenly serious. 'I really do, Emma.'

'Try not to interrupt – I'll find it easier to tell.'

'Understood.'

So I begin.

CHAPTER FOURTEEN

'I need to go back a long way, for this to make sense. As you probably know,' I say to Bruce, 'it was my grandmother who was the murder victim – my mother's mother. I called her Grandma Susie. I hadn't seen her since I was little, so I can't remember much about her; except that she was very tall and thin. Also, she had a very loud, snorty sort of laugh.

'Grandma Susie was once a famous actress – Susie Delacroix. Susie Delacroix was her stage name, not her real name. Her real name was Gladys Mungle.'

Bruce says, 'My mother still likes her old films.'

'They're not popular in our house … Anyway she went to live in Kalos ages ago, when my grandfather died. She more or less gave up the movie business or perhaps it gave her up. Her daughter – my mother – was just a baby. They'd all been there on holiday and fallen in love with the island. When she was widowed, Grandma had plenty of money. She wanted her daughter to grow up in sunshine, so the two of them left England to start a new life.'

'When are we talking about?' Bruce asks. 'How long ago?'

'Not exactly sure … maybe the early 1960s? It was all very undeveloped, not much tourism.'

'I'm with you so far,' Bruce says. 'Go on.'

'OK. So, Grandma Susie and my mother were lucky. They had no money worries and soon made plenty of friends. My grandmother spent her days having a good time – she used to run a lot too, it was her gimmick in the movies. She'd started as an athlete, a marathon runner, before she left England for Hollywood.'

'*Girl on the Run*, that's my mother's favourite,' Bruce says.

'It's her most famous, I think...Anyway, my mother went to the local school and Grandma gave her extra lessons in English and history, so she wouldn't forget her roots. I think they had a pretty good life. But, you have to understand that I really only know what my other grandmother, my Greek grandmother, told me about all this.

'Anyway, when my mother was eighteen she met my father Dino at a festival in Kalos town – that's the capital. Much to the disapproval of their parents, they got married three months later. My dad's Kaliot parents didn't approve because they'd seen too many "mixed marriages" fail. They thought my mother would have children, leave my father, go to England and that would be the last they'd see of their grandchildren. It sounds prejudiced but they'd seen divorces happen in other families where one partner was Greek and the other not.'

'Seems a bit harsh.'

'Maybe. Maybe just realistic. Anyway, Dad's parents were worried. And Grandma Susie was furious.'

'Why?'

'Well, whatever plans she had for my mother, they didn't include marrying a local boy, especially not someone like my father who was arty and dreamy. In those days he made jewellery and sold it on the beaches to the tourists.

'Despite the family objections, or maybe because of them, my mother and father stuck together. My father went away to Art College and my mother got work as one of the first holiday reps in the summer. Eventually they moved to London where my father hoped to be more successful as a jewellery designer, and he was.

'They still spent every spare moment they could in Kalos though, mostly with my dad's parents; they got used to their English daughter-in-law – I think they were quite close.

Grandma Susie still disapproved of the whole thing though.

'Then, ages later, my mother got pregnant – they'd been married a long time by then, so maybe I was an accident – I've wondered about that sometimes.

'I was born just before my Grandpa Spiro died. I think they probably hoped I'd be a boy, so I could be named after him. As it was, they gave me my grandmother's name as a middle name – I'm only thankful it's not my first name.'

'What is it? Something awful?'

'Persephone.'

'I think that's a beautiful name.'

'Maybe it is, in the right setting. It would not have gone down well in the playgrounds of Wandsworth, I can tell you that. Anyway, then when I was three, my mother died.'

'Bad break,' Bruce says. 'What she die of?'

'Hit-and-run driver.'

'Must have been horrible for you.'

I shake my head. 'Not really so horrible. Much worse for my father. I can't really remember her. I can't remember what it was like. I think losing a parent when you're older must be far worse. I mean, you were – what – twelve, when your dad died?'

Bruce nods.

'So you really knew him as a person. He's someone to miss. My mother dying wasn't really like that. Anyway, we went to stay with Grandma Persephone in Kalos for a while.'

'So what happened then?'

'We spent a lot of time there over the next few years. Grandma Susie was absolutely destroyed by my mum's death and she blamed my father, so we hardly ever saw her.'

'Why'd she blame your father?'

'My mother was crossing a dark street at night alone. She'd been to an evening class. My grandmother thought my dad should have picked her up from the college in the car; then it wouldn't have happened.'

'Not very fair. Did they get the driver?'

'No.'

'So then what?'

'Then after a bit Dad met Jan. She'd come to Kalos on holiday. She got on all right with his parents, but like Grandma Persephone says, she could never replace my mother.

'A few years ago I started to go to Kalos on holidays by myself. Dad would put me on the plane at Gatwick and Grandma Persephone would meet me at Kalos airport. I loved it.'

I stand up. 'Do you think we could go for a walk around? My leg's going to sleep.'

Bruce scrambles up. 'Sure.'

We set off round the outside of the cathedral, the afternoon turning cold.

'And then?' Bruce prompts.

'And then, out of the blue, just over two years ago, my father had a letter from Grandma Susie, saying she'd like to see him as soon as possible. It wasn't very convenient. He had a big exhibition coming up and things were a bit shaky, money-wise. Somehow he and Jan had built up quite a few debts. But he thought he ought to go, and he did.'

'So what did she want?'

'Seems she'd had a change of heart. She'd been going to leave all her money to an animal sanctuary or something but now she'd decided that her daughter's family should have it. Dad said he was surprised at the change in her. He thought she might be showing early signs of Alzheimer's.'

'Was she all by herself?'

'No. There'd been a sort of paid companion living with her for a while – no one knows for certain how long. She left just

80

a few days before my father got there.'

'English or Greek?'

'Don't know. No one from the family ever met her. Her name was Alexandra so she could have been either. Someone from the village said she had lovely long blonde hair. That's all I know.'

He nods.

'Anyway, Dad tried to make Grandma Susie think things over carefully, but she insisted that he drive her into town to change her will the very next day.'

'So we're relying on what your father says happened now?' I look at him sharply. 'What else do I have to go on?'

'OK. Just trying to get things clear in my head.'

We find an empty bench and sit down again.

'So then, she tells my father that she's tired of living, but she wants to come to England one last time. Thing is, she's frightened of planes. My father suggests she get some tranquillisers and drives her to the doctor to sort it out. The doctor's not too keen, but he agrees in the end. No sooner has she got the pills than she wants to be on the next possible plane, like there's no time to lose. Dad agrees to come back with her, even though he'd hoped to squeeze in some time with his own parents before returning to England.

'The night before they leave, Grandma's still terrified, despite the tablets. They decide to go to the taverna and ask the taxi to call for them there at midnight; the flight leaves really early in the morning.

'Dino phones Jan, and she and I are all set to meet them off the plane – I'm really excited. It's my chance to really get to know her – Jan's a bit less enthusiastic, unsurprisingly.

'So Grandma gets packed, has a couple of hours' sleep and they go to the taverna. They have a meal. She hardly eats anything but has a glass of brandy, maybe more than one, to steady her nerves. Dad tells her to take it easy, but he doesn't know how much she has to drink because he has to rush off to the loo, which is miles away.

'When he comes back he thinks she looks tired, suggests she's had enough and that they go back to her house, ask the taxi to call for them there instead. She doesn't want to and they argue. Dad has to run back to the loo again, his stomach's killing him. He's there for a while, and when he comes back, he can't see Grandma anywhere, so he assumes she must have gone to the airport without him. The taverna owner says the taxi came – it was early. We found out later it wasn't actually their taxi, though.

'Dad asks someone for a lift to the airport but they can't leave right away, so when they do eventually get there Dad has to run to board the plane on time. He's about to check with the steward about Grandma, he can't see her anywhere, but he suddenly feels really sick and by the time he's recovered, they're in the air.'

'Didn't they have adjoining seats?' Bruce says.

'What?'

'Wouldn't their tickets have been for two seats together?'

'Apparently not. They were last minute, ultra-cheap tickets. Dad was hoping they could sort it out at the airport so he could sit next to Grandma on the flight...but it didn't happen.'

'Right.'

'So then,' I say, 'Dad tries to find her. He has to divert to the loo again before he sees the steward and, while he's in there, he collapses. The next thing he remembers is landing at Gatwick.'

'And your grandmother?'

I pause, looking down at the bare patch of earth by my foot.

'She never got on the plane. She died in Kalos, at the bottom of a cliff.'

'And what did the post mortem say, Emma?'

'She died of an overdose of drugs and drink and the fall.'

'And they suspected…' Bruce puts his hand on mine.

'Yes!' I suddenly shout. 'They thought Dad had got her drunk, drugged her up, pushed her over a cliff and jumped on the next plane!'

An elderly couple with a little white dog look startled and steer a course away from us.

'Of course they didn't say all that in public, but they thought the circumstances were suspicious – of course they were suspicious – people might get drunk or off their faces on drugs but they don't usually jump off cliffs. So the police started a full investigation. At first,' I say, 'they couldn't establish a motive. But of course it didn't take them five minutes to discover that Dad stood to inherit all Grandma Susie's money. The fact that he wouldn't hurt a fly and was, like, really upset when her body was discovered, made no difference. And the guy who found her said she called out Dino's name – that made it look bad.'

I'm shivering now and Bruce puts his arm round me.

'They believed him, though,' Bruce says. 'He was found not guilty. Is the Greek system the same as ours?'

'Not really, they have this thing called the Court of First Instance and – well, anyway, all that's not important. It's not even that I blame them. Dino had MMO – he'd have been under suspicion in any country where it happened I suppose.'

'MMO?'

'Means, motive, opportunity.'

'Of course. Sorry. They cleared him though – right?'

'It took them long enough – fifteen and a half hours. And whatever the court thought, some people had other ideas, including Grandma Persephone. His own mother thinks he might have done it. Which is why I'm not allowed to go to Kalos any more. After the court case she sold her story to the English tabloids: "WAS MY SON THE SLAYER OF A SCREEN LEGEND?"'

'You know what the papers are like – they probably twisted what she said.'

'She didn't have to talk to them at all. They were out for blood and headlines. Someone had to pay for Susie Delacroix's death, and as there were no other suspects...'

We're silent for a bit. There are gulls circling the spire. It must be rough at sea.

'We get phone calls,' I say.

'Who from?'

'All sorts. People who claim to be Grandma Susie's biggest fans ... I didn't even know she had a fan club until she died – and there's loads about her on the internet.'

Bruce hugs me. 'Thanks for telling me. I can see it wasn't easy – you look tired.'

'I'm OK. I'm glad you know it all now.'

'Let's get a coffee before we go home,' Bruce says. 'I'm freezing.'

We find a burger bar. Bruce has a cheeseburger, but I'm not hungry.

On the way to the bus station I lean against his shoulder, sorry that I won't be able to see him again properly until next weekend.

'Emma,' he says, 'do you want to go to Kalos again?'

'Of course, one day. But—'

'Shut up a minute. I've thought of a way we can rescue our

84

summer holidays. I've been thinking about this for a while, actually.'

'Go on.'

'I think that you and I should go to Kalos. I've always wanted to go to Greece anyway – and we might be able to find out what really happened to your grandmother; clear your father's name?'

'They'll never let us,' I say. 'Great idea, Bruce, but...'

'What if it's for our heducashun?'

'What do you mean?'

He sighs. 'Don't you ever read the School Bulletin?'

'Not unless I'm more bored than anyone in the whole history of boredom has ever been – why?'

He pulls a neatly folded piece of paper from the back pocket of his jeans and gives it to me. 'You can read it while we're waiting for the bus. You can skip the stuff about triumphs on the sports field.'

'Phew!'

'Just read it, Emma.'

So I sit on the cold bench and read. And this is what it says:

INVESTIGATING CLIMATE CHANGE – A FIELD TRIP

Many of you will know that the popular TV natural historian David Bradley was formerly a student at Hillingbury.

Six years ago, Dave opened an ecology study centre on the Greek island of Kalos in the Ionian sea. He has provided Hillingbury students with discounted rates ever since.

This year's trip is to study coastal erosion and wildlife habitats. Anyone in Years 9, 10 and 11 may apply to go and participating students in Years 10 and 11 will earn credits

85

in the Project Neptune Scheme.

The trip will be from July 16th – 23rd. Hostel accommodation and most meals will be provided. Four teachers (TBC) will accompany our students: Vincent Clayton (Science), Gregory Southgate (Geography), Rebecca Gumn (Science) and Charlotte Stone (PE).

Numbers are limited and we expect the trip to be oversubscribed. Should that be the case, any students who have participated in previous years will not be included in the draw for places.

The cost of the trip is £280.00 to include return flights from Gatwick Airport.

Please note that while we are happy for students to meet up with their parents for a family holiday in Kalos after the trip, no refunds for non-used return portions of flight tickets can be made and in addition the airline may make an additional charge as all flights must be booked by the school on a return basis. We would ask that parents do NOT book holidays to Kalos to run concurrently with the trip, as we have found from experience that this can be very distracting... blah blah blah de blah blah.

'What do you think, Em? Should we try to go?'

I throw my arms around him.

'Absolutely completely one hundred per cent... YES!'

Can I do it? Yes, I just have to be brave and go for it. Whatever happens, things can't stay like this. Bruce and I decide we'll have to stay on in Kalos after the trip – there won't be much chance for sleuthing otherwise.

So Bruce tells Hamish that he wants to go on the school trip and afterwards do some work for a conservation project, which means he won't be able to see his mother after all.

We both agree that our 'cover destination' should be Rhodes. We don't want to run the risk of Hamish making a connection between the trip and me, or my father. Bruce even gets his mother to cough up some dosh.

'How did she take it?' I ask as we sit in the school library, surreptitiously eating M&Ms. 'The fact that you won't be coming to Crawley?'

'She pretended to be disappointed,' Bruce says. 'But of course she was really pleased. No one can accuse her of being a bad mother now – she asked me to visit; I had a school trip and a project to do which meant that I couldn't. When I hinted that there might be some difficulty over dosh she told me to hang on for a minute. Then she came back and said would a cheque for three hundred quid help?'

'Wow. Talk about lucky.'

'Exactly. Obviously the thought that I might still land up on her doorstep due to lack of funds was enough to scare her into sending me this.'

He fishes in his bag and waves the cheque triumphantly. 'I can't help but notice that it's signed by the boyfriend, but hey, I'm not proud. The weird thing is how Hamish didn't kick off. I actually think that, even though I'm not going to be available as cheap labour in the shop, he's secretly pleased I'm not going to be spending time with my mother.'

'I only hope I find it so easy,' I say.

CHAPTER FIFTEEN

I don't.

I make notes about what I have to do. Cancel the visit to Aunty Chris. Cancel the trip to the Dordogne. Get enough money. Think.

I think about just not turning up at Aunty Chris's house, but she'd probably alert Interpol, which might spoil Dad and Jan's holiday somewhat.

In the end I decide I'll have to lie. There is no other way.

'Jan,' I say, one day after school.

She's lying on a sunbed in the back garden, trying to build up a tan for summer. I sometimes wonder if she's even heard of the hole in the ozone layer.

She's reading a book about France: *101 Ways With Snails*, possibly? I bring her out a cup of tea. Dino's in the workshop, being creative – I hope.

'Jan?'

'Hmmm? Oh, thank you, Em. Nice cup of tea.'

I smile. 'Could I talk to you?'

'Of course.' She puts on her concerned parent expression, no doubt hoping for something juicy, maybe about sex or drugs.

I sit next to her on the grass. Deep breath. 'I was wondering if you'd mind if I went on a school trip this summer, to Rhodes, instead of going to Aunty Chris and the Dordogne?'

There's silence for a moment, then: 'What kind of trip?' she asks.

I explain all about Project Neptune and how I've only recently got interested in it and how the school trip counts towards it – and of course I tell her I'll be gone for four weeks.

'Sounds wonderful,' she says. 'I expect your teachers will be pleased to see you getting stuck in to school life, becoming involved with things.'

'Maybe.'

'Are you sure you can spare the time away from your studying? Four weeks is a heck of a long time. I mean Global Warming is all very well; but is it part of your GCSE curriculum?'

'Jan – it should be a part of everyone's curriculum,' I say seriously. 'And Mr Hampton says that participation in Project Neptune looks good on our CVs.'

Jan frowns. 'Where's the note about the trip?'

'Er, I expect Dino lost it – you know what he's like.'

'I've told you before,' Jan says, 'anything important from school, give it to me, not your dad. You know he's hopeless when it comes to paperwork.'

'Sure. Sorry.'

'So how much is this going to cost us then?'

I daren't look directly at her. 'About three hundred pounds. I'll need some spending money while I'm there but I've got some dosh in my savings account I can use too.'

She looks doubtful. 'I'm not sure . . .'

'You can make it my birthday present, if you like,' I say. 'I mean I know it's more than you'd usually spend. What I mean is, I'll do without a birthday present, if it'll help.'

'That's OK,' Jan says. 'It actually sounds extremely reasonable, for four weeks. It is a very long trip – I'm surprised that the staff are willing to give up so much of their holidays. But then I suppose Rhodes is an attractive destination . . .'

'So can I go?'

'I'll have to talk it over with your dad. We both wanted you to come to the Dordogne, see it for yourself before we make any major decisions.'

'You're still thinking of moving there?' I say.

Jan sighs. 'Yes, Emma. I think we badly need a new start. Somewhere where the name Dino Xenos means nothing – except fine jewellery.'

Sometimes I think Jan is quite mad.

'And Emma?'

'Yes?'

'You'll need to find that note.'

Damn.

I hate having to lie to them and I'm surprised at how easily it can be done. I'm unreasonably worried that Dad, or more likely Jan, will mention the details of the school trip to someone in the village and we'll get found out. For once I'm quite glad that they're Mr and Mrs No-Mates round here.

I don't know if Bruce feels bad about deceiving Hamish; somehow, we don't talk about that.

We work on the problem of the note together, using Bruce's computer. It's not as difficult as I first thought. We simply scan in the note, change Kalos to Rhodes, delete the reference to David Bradley's study centre – which they may have heard of – and change the end date. I give the new, improved version to Jan as she's cleaning her brushes. There's a new colour in her paintings – green.

She reads through it while I hold my breath and put the kettle on, trying to look as if I'm thinking about something else.

'Unbelievable,' she says at last.

My hand shakes as I pour boiling water into the teapot, 'How do you mean?' I try to sound casual.

'You'd think someone as supposedly educated as your headmaster would know that Rhodes is part of the Dodecanese, not the Ionian islands.'

90

'Right.'

Whoops!

'And who in their right minds would want to join their children for a holiday after the kids have already spent four weeks in Greece? The little dears will be going native by then I shouldn't wonder.'

'I don't think many people will bother,' I say hastily.

'I'll speak to your dad about it tonight,' she says.

That night I hear them arguing – they hardly ever do. I get out of bed and sit on the floor by the door, trying to make out what they're saying.

'It's not safe!' Dino's voice is raised. 'It's not safe for her to go there!'

'For God's sake, Dino, it's a school trip. They'll have four teachers with them. And it's Rhodes we're talking about, not Rio de bloody Janeiro!!'

'She's too young to be away from me – from us.'

'She's not a baby any more – I think we should burbleburbletwurbleburble – it's a...burble...integrate... twurble...peers.'

'From what I see, most of them are not good enough for her time of day. Shit on her shoe.'

This surprises me. Not the poor English – like I say, Dino's language skills slip if he's tired or upset – but the fact that he's noticed.

'Twurbleburble. Cotton wool.'

I can't hear any more, so I tiptoe back to bed. I can't sleep. What will they decide? I think I'll die if they don't let me go.

CHAPTER SIXTEEN

The next day is bright and sunny and almost warm. I take it as an omen.

'Did you have a chance to talk to Dad about the school trip yet?' I ask Jan as casually as I can.

She sighs and puts down her toast. 'I have to say he has reservations, Emma. He has this feeling that something bad will happen to you if you go – but I think I've managed to persuade him.'

'Thank you, Jan.' I can't stop smiling. I get up and hug her. 'You don't know what it means to me.'

'I can guess.'

Oh hell – can she? I try not to let my face fall.

'Is there, by any chance, a young man by the name of Bruce Brown going on this trip?'

Phew. 'I'm – er – not sure. I—'

Luckily the phone rings and Jan goes to answer it – it's another call from a member of the fan club; they don't usually bother this early in the day. Jan comes back, grim-faced.

'I'll have to get on to BT about changing the number – again.'

As soon as she's off the phone, I'm on it to Bruce.

'I can go, I can go!'

'Excellent. Now we just have to hope we both get selected.'

'How do you mean?'

'I've heard too many people want to go, including our best pals, Megan and Katie.'

'I don't care who's going, just as long as we are.'

As I approach the school gates on Monday, I see several trees and a telegraph pole have phone photos pinned to them, taken

92

when we had the playground fight. They look even worse enlarged. I look completely crazy, Megan looks really scared. Underneath one of them someone's written: STAY AWAY FROM THE KILLERS DAUGHTER, OTHERWISE THERE MIGHT BE A SLAUGHTER.

It doesn't scan very well. I bet they had to look up how to spell slaughter.

Inside the school there are several more posters in various locations. Some of the photos are better than others – in one it looks like I'm trying to kiss Megan – eeuw.

Other slogans include WATCH OUT THERES A KILLER ABOUT. And LIKE FATHER LIKE DORTA. And THIS GIRL IS EXTREEMLEY DANGERUS – BWARE.

By lunch time the ones inside the school have all been taken away, though everyone seems to be laughing and talking about them.

A few days later and there's bad news. Bruce is right, the school trip to Kalos is oversubscribed; forty-two people chasing thirty places. There's to be a draw in the hall after school on Friday. Everyone who wants to go has to be there. Bruce and I sit at the front. He holds my hand until Miss Stone comes in and frowns at us. Mr Clayton is with her – he's carrying a large, floppy, pointed hat.

'This isn't Hogwarts, sir,' Bruce says. 'It's too late to sort us now.'

Several people laugh.

'Thanks for pointing that out, Bruce,' Mr Clayton says.

'Can I be in Slytherin?' someone shouts from the back.

Mr Clayton sighs. 'It's Mr Hampton's idea,' he says. 'He wanted you all to see that it's all fair and above board – no favouritism. You've probably all guessed that your names are in this hat. I'll draw thirty of them out and Miss Stone will write the names on a list that will then be pinned up in reception – all clear?'

We nod. The tension mounts. Megan Marsh and Katie Cooper are sitting behind us. I'm surprised they want to go.

'Who knew they'd be interested in climate change?' I whisper to Bruce.

'I think it's more likely they're interested in suntans and Greek boys and getting off school for the last few days of term.'

'You're probably right. I just hope they don't get picked.'

Mr Clayton starts:

'Sam Walkersmart, Harry Eaton, Duncanna Jennings, Charlie Sonnenberg, Georgia Crook, Leroy Saunders, Bruce Brown, Katie Cooper, Pete Roth, Stacey Austin, Kate Lusher, Wayne Chang, Serena Turton, Robert Garfield, Nina Dalton, Peter Oldaker, Jordan Oak, Jennie Brown-Windsor, Lee Ansty, Ellie Salter, William Bradley, Jack Bradley – what are the chances? – Sophie Blandford, Tommy Toomer, Megan Marsh, Alexander Waits, Georgia Nadal...'

Only three more left... oh please oh please oh please.

'Ali McBride – I can't read this one.' He shows it to Miss Stone.

'Chloe-Elisabeth Buckley.' She writes it on the list.

'And the last one is...'

Bruce is gripping my hand again tightly, I feel like I want to be sick.

'Emma Egg-zee-noss.' Mr Clayton looks straight at me. 'Sorry, my pronunciation...'

'That's OK.' I can hardly breathe.

'Anyone here today whose name hasn't been read out will be put on the waiting – what is it, Megan?'

'She can't come – you can't let her come.' She taps me on the back with one bony finger.

'Don't be silly, Megan. What d'you mean?'

'She'll kill us all – don't you know her father's a murderer? She's a killer's daughter... And she's a dyke – her hair proves it.'

I swing round and slap her hard on her stupid face. It makes a great thwacking noise, it even echoes slightly.

On Monday I make my way to Hampton's office. At my old school, nearly all crimes and misdemeanours were dealt with by Year Heads. Unluckily for me, Hampton believes in being a hands-on head teacher. He even teaches history to some classes – luckily not mine though.

Henry Hampton the Hellish Head of Hillingbury High Hails History Ha Ha. I repeat this mantra several times to myself as I trudge up the familiar stairs.

I knock and go in. Miss Stone is with him, which I hope is a good sign.

'Take a seat,' says Hampton. 'You know why you're here?'

I shrug. 'I guess.'

'In view of this incident, we may have to reconsider your place on the trip.'

I have to make a huge effort. The room seems unnaturally bright.

'Please let me go,' I say. 'I could be useful – I can speak Greek quite well.'

'Language skills are not the issue,' Hampton says. 'Why did you hit another pupil? How do we know you won't assault someone else on foreign soil?'

'I hit Megan Marsh because she called my father a murderer – you were there.' I turn to Miss Stone.

She looks uncomfortable. 'We've interviewed Megan this morning. She's told us she's actually very frightened of you and if you go on the trip she'll feel scared.'

'She'll feel scared?'

'There was the playground incident and she says you've often threatened her verbally, even threatened to kill her.'

'She's a liar.'

How can I explain? I want to just get up and walk out, like last time. But I don't because if I do I can kiss goodbye to any chance of seeing Kalos. Tears prick my eyes but I blink them away. My face feels hot.

'Ever since I started here,' I say, 'Megan and her little gang have had it in for me and I...'

'It seems to me,' Hampton interrupts, 'that once again, it's six of one and half a dozen of the other.'

'It really isn't,' I say. 'If only you knew what's been...'

'Your best plan is to keep quiet,' Hampton says. 'Megan has admitted her culpability, her verbal abuse of you yesterday—'

Miss Stone interrupts. 'She used inappropriate and homo-phobic language...'

'Homophobic?'

Hampton frowns at Miss Stone but she ignores him. 'She called you a dyke. Your sexuality is no one's business but your own. Homophobic behaviour is not tolerated in this school – any more than racism.'

I stare at her. 'She called me a killer's daughter—'

'But you must understand, Emma, she sees you as a real threat.'

I can't believe I'm hearing this. I'm about to pipe up again when Hampton raises his hand.

'One more chance,' he says. 'Against my better judgement, but I'll give you one more chance. It seems to be your ineluctable fate to be sitting here in my office, Emma, and I don't want you inhabiting that chair again. Now, will you agree to shake Megan's hand and try to let bygones be bygones?'

I nod. To get to Kalos I'd go line dancing with Hitler.

That night Bruce and I get on our PCs and forge letters from our 'rents, saying that they'll be joining us on Kalos for a holiday when the trip's over. We know that anyone wanting to do that has to meet up at Kalos Airport before the school takes the return flight home – but we'll worry about how to get round that later. For now it seems we're all set.

Ineluctable. Now there's a worthy Word of the Week.

CHAPTER SEVENTEEN

It's my birthday. Bruce has thrown caution to the wind and come over. This afternoon we're going to Bournemouth to see John T's latest at the Odeon and then fish and chips at Harry Ramsden's. Dino is chauffeuring us both ways as there's an exhibition of modern art and sculpture that he and Jan want to see. I've sort of implied that there might be others from school meeting up with us, without actually lying as such. Who am I kidding? Bruce and I have agreed it's not a good idea if either lot of 'rents suspect that we're seeing so much of each other. Of course I'm still officially off-limits to Bruce anyway, as far as Hamish is concerned.

Anyway, Bruce arrives about eleven just as Dad and Jan are getting up. They make coffee and watch me unwrap my present from Bruce. It's a simple painting of two figures in a small blue and white fishing boat. It's unmistakeably Greece – peaceful and beautiful. There's a backdrop of dark green hills and clear blue sea under a cloudless sky.

'Thank you,' I whisper. 'This is so awesome.'

Dino looks, his eyes widen. 'This is very good,' he says. 'You study art at school, Bruce?'

'No. It's just a hobby.'

'Where is it?' I say. 'Cephalonia again?'

He taps the side of his head. 'Nope. I made this one up.'

'Have you been to Greece?' Jan asks.

'Not yet, but of course I'll be going to Kalos next month.'

My stomach turns over. He realises what he's said.

'I mean Rhodes,' he adds quickly. 'I'll be going to Rhodes,' he laughs maniacally. They must think he's insane.

There's a pause while Jan pours more coffee. I can see she's perplexed by this remark.

Dino looks amused. 'You know of course that I am from Kalos – and that Emma is half Greek?'

Bruce gulps his coffee. 'She's mentioned it.'

'I like to paint...' Jan says, lighting a cigarette.

I frown at her.

'You will love Greece,' Dino says. 'The light is wonderful for a painter.'

Jan thrusts a package into my hands. 'Happy Birthday to You!' she sings.

It's wrapped in silver hologram paper – dead expensive. The card says: To our dearest Emma, with lots of love from Dad and Jan xxxx

Jan's written it, though Dad's signed his name. I'm choked.

'I thought we agreed I wasn't having a present – because of the school trip.'

Jan smiles. 'We bought it before, when you were coming to France – I thought it'd be nice for you to have something new to wear – but I guess you can wear it in Rhodes just as well.'

I open it slowly. Inside is a dead cool pair of ice-blue cropped trousers with a matching sleeveless top splattered in silver. There's also a brand new dark blue and silver swimsuit.

'Thanks,' I say. 'They're perfect.' I push my fist into my eyes; suddenly I feel very emotional.

There's a card from Kalos. Grandma Persephone has sent me fifty euros. Inside the card (donkeys in an olive grove) she's written: Hope you have a happy birthday – I miss you so much.

There's a bit of an atmosphere as Dino looks at Jan and Jan looks at Dino and Bruce looks at the floor, and I'm glad there's one more present to open. It's from my Aunt Chris, an XXL sweatshirt in salmon pink, adorned with the head of a rather belligerent-looking Pekinese. It's so breathtakingly hideous that we're all temporarily dumbstruck. Then I start to laugh and the others join in and then everything's OK again.

'There's a card, too,' Jan says.

I open it. It has a picture of another, somewhat less fierce Pekinese on the front. The message inside says: Hope your birthday finds you at the Peke of happiness.

When we're alone I say to Bruce, 'I can't believe you nearly blew it. I thought you were supposed to be a genius.'

'I am a genius. Mozart, Einstein, Hawking and Hammett didn't – or don't – have to think about practical matters like clandestine trips abroad and how to go about them.'

'Who the hell is Hammett?'

'Metallica's lead guitarist. Have I taught you nothing, girl?'

'Of course – should have known. You can test me on Metallica later, after I've had a chance to revise.'

'Oh shut up, Emma.'

'Make me.'

He does so, by kissing me. We're getting better at it.

The rest of the term passes in a blur of end-of-term exams, various sporting tournaments, field trips and OH NO! WORK EXPERIENCE, which is horrendous as I stupidly didn't do anything about it until all the good stuff was gone. I end up spending a fortnight working for an alcoholic travel agent in Dinsbury. The only advantage of this being not much work and plenty of time online to catch up with all the latest on John T. Bruce gets a plum placement at some design consultancy 'Up That London'.

I can hardly believe it but I've had a letter from Surrinder, my old friend from Wandsworth – no idea how she got my address. She tells me she's getting married to someone called Jas whom she met at Temple.

Jas looks handsome in a conventional kind of way – but he's much too old for Surrinder. Surrinder looks unbearably smug. I wonder what happened to her plans to work for Médecins Sans Frontières.

It's the very last days of Year 10. Those of us going on the trip are leaving at the end of the week. Some people are actually crying.

'Are they demented or what?' I say to Stace. 'We'll all be back here in September – for the dreaded Year 11.'

We're standing in the playground, shivering in the northerly breeze and the drizzle. Another wonderful English summer.

'I don't think they're crying about the end of term. I think they're crying about Megan Marsh,' she says.

'Why? She been beating people up again?'

'No, Emma, she was attacked – she's in a coma.'

'Wow,' I say slowly. 'How did that happen?'

Before Stace can reply, Katie Cooper comes over. Her face is flushed but she doesn't look like she's been crying.

'I'm sorry to hear about Megan,' I say to her. It's true, I am. I mean I hate them both, but you wouldn't wish that on anyone. 'Will she be OK?'

'Cut the crap,' she hisses. 'Just tell me where your father was last night!'

'What? I dunno...at home – in his workshop...why?'

'Because, Killer's Daughter, Megan was pushed off Blackbeam Bridge – it's just like when he pushed that old actress off that cliff.'

I'm too dumbstruck to say anything. I just want to put my hands over my ears and scream and scream. I don't though. I just turn away and run inside the science block.

'They'll get your father!' Katie yells after me. 'He won't get away with it this time!'

CHAPTER EIGHTEEN

I see Bruce at lunch time, in the library.

'I heard what happened this morning,' he says. 'Stupid girl. Still, I suppose she was upset.'

I nod, biting my lip. 'It's just made me more determined than ever to get to Kalos, to find out what really happened.'

We risk a hug, thinking there's no one about, but Miss Read's voice booms out loud and clear:

'This library does not have a Romance section; kindly keep your hands to yourselves.'

Bruce tells me later he's heard that Megan is really ill; she might even die. All sorts of rumours are going round. Of course she can't come on the trip to Kalos now. I think about where Dad was last night. He was in his workshop until about nine, then he went for a walk by himself – to clear his head, he said – while Jan watched TV and I read. He didn't come back until after I'd gone to bed. Blackbeam bridge, where Megan got hurt, is in Blackbeam Woods – quite near our house. I wonder if he might have seen anything. I think about the way he looked at Megan, that day when he had to come into school.

I remember when I told him how made up I was to get a place on the school trip, but how I wished Megan Marsh wasn't coming too; she'd spoil the landscape. We'd laughed and he'd said maybe something would happen in the meantime so she couldn't go, but if it didn't:

'You must keep your distance, she is bad newspaper, that girl.'

On the way to the airport in the coach I read about John's next film project.

'How can you?' Bruce says. 'It'd make me sick.'

We've been up since before the dawn chorus had finished and are both feeling slightly unreal. I had a nasty moment the night before when Jan offered to come and see me off.

'I love airports,' she said wistfully. 'They're so exciting – all those people with their different stories flying who-knows-where. Perhaps I could get up and give you a lift to school at least.' She sounded doubtful. 'Though it is rather an early start. You know me, not really a morning person.'

'I'd rather you didn't,' I said. 'No one else's mum's coming.'

She smiled at me. 'Thank you,' she says.

'For what?'

'For acknowledging me as your mum.'

Actually that isn't what I'd meant at all. It's a funny thing, considering how young I was when my mother died, but I've never really thought of Jan as my mum. I didn't even know that she wanted me to. She's always been Dad's wife first, and being a parent to me just sort of came as part of the package, so I thought.

Feeling rather awkward, I gave her a hug.

'Emma,' she said, 'you will be careful, won't you?'

'Of course,' I said.

'We want lots of postcards!' Dino yelled from the bathroom.

Now that could be a problem.

The local paper, which I read while we bump and sway along the motorway, says that Megan Marsh was: 'Attacked by an unknown assailant while walking home through Blackbeam Wood.'

It goes on: 'She has woken from her coma though is still said by her mother to be "very weak". Megan was able to describe her attacker as a dark man in his late forties or early fifties, wearing a white T-shirt and jeans. The motive remains a mystery. Although her purse containing approximately £5.60 has gone missing, the police do not think robbery was the primary motive for this savage attack on a young and defenceless teenage girl. Megan's mother was reported to be too upset to comment further.'

'Strange,' I say to Bruce.

But he's slowly turning green.

'Why didn't you take some travel sickness tablets?' I say, somewhat impatiently.

'I thought I'd save them for the plane.'

I find my bottle of water and fumble around in his bag for the tablets.

'Take them now,' I say. 'We could walk to Kalos in the time it's taking this coach to get to the airport.'

So many shops, so little time. I suppose it's because I've been stuck in the depths of the countryside, but I'm quite dazzled by all the opportunities to spend money at the airport. I've always wanted a pink bandana...

'Don't,' Bruce says firmly. 'We haven't got that much between us. We don't know how long it's got to last.'

He's looking a little less like the living dead since we got off the coach and the travel sickness tablets have kicked in.

'I've told you,' I say. 'We'll stay with my grandmother – it won't cost us anything.'

'Keep together,' yells Mr Clayton. 'Hillingbury High students – don't wander off.'

He goes over to one of the departure screens. 'Time to go,' he says. So the question of to buy or not to buy is taken out of my hands.

We're just about to pass the final checkpoint and proceed on board when the flight-checker person, or whatever she's called, says something to Bruce.

'Just a minute.' She's looking at his passport and back at him and back at his passport again. We wait, frozen, while the rest of our party swarm past us and into their seats.

'Is this really you?' she says at last.

I can't believe it – she's smiling.

'About time you had this updated, isn't it?'

She's flirting with him – am I dreaming?

Bruce smiles back. 'I really must get around to it,' he says.

And that's it and suddenly we're in our seats and there's horrible Easy Listening playing, which is supposed to relax you but which makes me want to break all the windows.

'Please let me have your passports back on arrival in Kalos,' Mr Clayton says. 'I don't want anyone to lose them or there'll be hell to pay. And those lucky ducks meeting up with parents to continue your stay on the island, make sure you get them back from me before the end of the trip.' He seems in a very happy mood. Perhaps it's because he's sitting with Miss Stone.

I let Bruce have the window seat. I hope it'll be clear all the way across.

I grab his passport off him before he slips it into his pocket.

'Gissa look at that photo.'

He looks about ten years old – quite sweet really.

CHAPTER NINETEEN

Green spikes rush up to meet us as the plane makes its final descent onto the alarmingly small airstrip. 'Cypress trees,' I whisper to Bruce. Suddenly, stupidly, I want to cry.

I feel like I've come home.

I'd forgotten the heat. Some people describe it as a wall. The wall of heat that hits you as you leave the plane. I think of it more as a blanket which wraps you up and warms you to the bone, so you feel as though you could never be cold again.

'It's a bit hot,' Bruce says unnecessarily.

We stand in the airless terminal watching the empty carousel turning, waiting for our backpacks to show up. Everyone is quiet, as if waiting for a sound from the bowels of the building that might herald the arrival of the luggage.

Lots of people are smoking – I suppose because they couldn't do it on the plane and because on this island the non-smokers are the oddities. Even Mr Clayton has lit up – not a good example.

Then – here it comes – and everyone's scrabbling for their luggage. We grab our bags and get swept up in a flock who are being herded towards their coach by a brightly painted holiday rep. She's wearing a luminous pink suit with matching hideous hat bearing the word 'GOODTIMERS'.

'Everyone for Aggy-Yarney, this way please,' she booms. She has the looks and the voice of someone not to be messed with.

'Is that a place or an activity?' Bruce giggles.

'It's a blot on the landscape – a hideous resort. Actually though, it's not too far from Gran's house.'

We find our coach and soon we're on our way. Once clear of the airport, some of our travelling companions sing lame songs:

106

'Ten Green Bottles'? Please no. A few people have iPods. Bruce and I sit and hold hands. We gaze and gaze out the windows at the beautiful, breathtaking, brilliant world outside. As the road starts to climb, we look down through sun-painted olive trees, their trunks so ancient and twisted they're like something from a fairy tale. There's an old woman dressed in traditional black with a sweet-faced donkey loaded up with forage.

A crazy man rides his kamikaze scooter round us on a blind bend, making the coach driver brake and swear. On the hills are more dark green cypress spears. The road is by turn orange and dusty, then grey and shiny – either seems to suit the driver who steers the coach over steep hills and crumbling tarmac with impressive speed and nonchalance. Hanging from his rear view mirror is a little plastic saint, there to protect us against RTAs – though there were no such things when the saint was actually alive.

By the roadside are little glass-fronted boxes on sticks – some burning oil lamps, some with pictures or statuettes or both of this same saint.

Here and there are houses. Some old, painted brilliant white, their windows blue-shuttered against the sun. There are others in pale terracotta, fronted by large tins that once contained olive oil, now serving as patio pots. Then there are the newer ones, their flat roofs growing giant metal hairpins – unfinished because of tax, so Grandma Persephone used to tell me. The hairpins are actually reinforcing rods, because of the risk of earthquakes. On old and new houses alike, the purple and pink bougainvillea climbs towards clear sky. It's about as far from the Wilds of Wessex as Mars.

'Is it like you imagined?' I ask.

I can't help noticing Bruce is turning green again.

*

Before we came here, I thought that the week we'd have to spend with the school party would be something to be got through before Bruce and I could be free. But actually, I quite enjoy it. The teachers are much more relaxed than they are in school. It's quite sweet watching Mr Clayton's budding romance with Miss Stone and the field trips are really interesting. We get taken to parts of the island I haven't seen before. At one place the coastal erosion has caused part of the cliffs to break away into magical towers and bridges. They look really solid but are fragile sandstone. In a few years' time, they'll be gone. I sit next to Bruce while he sketches them.

'Like something out of a fairy tale,' I say.

'Perhaps I should draw Mordor next to one of them.'

'You can be so dumb.'

'Dumb yourself – your nose is going pink.'

At night we sleep in dormitories. There are five girls in mine – and I could scream when I find Katie Cooper is one of them – though she keeps her distance. The first night I can hear her crying. Someone gets up to ask her what's wrong.

'Nothing – I'm just homesick and it's so hot and I'm worried about Megan and I forgot to bring my moisturiser.'

'I'll lend you some,' says the voice kindly.

'Is it – is it Clarins?'

'What's Clarins? It's Boots or Tesco own brand – I think. My mum got it for me.'

More crying – what a wimp.

'I've got plenty of moisturiser,' I say to no one in particular. 'If anyone needs any . . .'

It's true I have. Jan loaded me up with industrial quantities of something weird and organic. There's a small pause, then: 'Don't touch it, anyone,' Katie hisses. 'It'll be poisoned.'

I roll over. A bit surprised to find I don't much care. It's something about being here; the heat and the light. Everything seems clearer, brighter and at the same time softer, which seems like a contradiction. Just part of the magic of Kalos I guess.

I mutter a small incantation in Greek. (I've hardly spoken Greek since we've been here, mainly because I've forgotten so much, but I like to show off what I do know to my delightful fellow travellers.) A rough translation:

'Katie Cooper is a goat. Her mother is a goat. Her father is a goat. Grandparents and great-grandparents on both sides were goats. I hope she falls down a mountain face-first into a humungous hill of goat shit.'

'What's she saying?' someone asks sleepily.

'Nothing – just my prayers,' I say.

But Katie cheers up the next day when she gets talking to a barman she meets at a beach bar where we go for a drink. (It's too hot to do much about global warming in the afternoons.) The day after that, she's absent from our field trip to a wetland site – supposedly ill. Miss Stone offers to stay with her but she insists she'll be OK. When we return to the hostel later, she's mysteriously better and after that she often goes missing.

The week goes really quickly. On the last night all the teachers take us to a karaoke bar.

Bruce nudges me. 'Look over there, at Katie.'

She's eating the face off the barman she's met. Miss Stone notices too and goes over to speak to her. Bruce and I move closer to listen.

'Will you excuse us a moment, please?' she says to the barman.

He shrugs and whispers something in Katie's ear. She giggles. Then he gets up and heads to the bar.

'Katie,' says Miss Stone. 'You should be with the rest of the group, not kissing handsome young Greeks.'

'He's not Greek, he's Albanian.'

Miss Stone rolls her eyes. 'Whatever. Look, this is a school trip. We don't want to be killjoys, but holiday romances were not supposed to be on the agenda – and you have to remember that the other teachers and I are in *loco parentis*...what would your mother think if she could have seen you just now with that young man's tongue down your throat?'

'I don't care how loco you are – and my mother wouldn't mind – she'd be pleased for me. Ashpet comes from a really rich family – his father owns hotels all over Albania. Ashpet's going to run them when he's older.'

'Ask yourself then, Katie, what he's doing as a barman on Kalos?'

'Well, durr, work experience, miss?'

'That's as maybe – but we're going home tomorrow...'

'So? I'm going to Albania after my GCSEs – Ashpet says I can live with his family. Albania sounds really cool. Better than England anyway.'

'Do you even know where Albania is, Katie?'

Now it's Katie's turn to roll her eyes. 'Well, of course I do. It's near the Caribbean – you're just jealous.'

Miss Stone gives up. 'Just be careful, Katie. And – er – don't forget you're underage.'

'Not in Albania, I wouldn't be.'

'The innocence of some teachers can be quite touching,' Bruce whispers to me.

Miss Stone returns to the group. As the evening goes on, the teachers drink too much and Mr Clayton does some dirty dancing with Miss Stone. He looks up at her adoringly when she gets up to sing 'Hips Don't Lie'.

Truly tragic.

Miss Gumn tries to do her sudoku puzzles but is eventually persuaded to perform 'Moondance'. Clearly she's had far more retsina than anyone has realised. Mr Southgate listens to his iPod and stays glued to his chair.

CHAPTER TWENTY

The next morning I feel tense and sick. We have to get this right. Along with four others, Bruce and I are meeting up with our parents at the airport while the rest of the party fly back to England. Only of course, in our case, there are no parents. I'm just hoping we can pull it off.

We get lucky when we discover that Katie Cooper has overslept. Nobody's woken her and she's so slow getting her stuff together and saying goodbye to Albanian Ashpet that she nearly misses the coach – making the teachers flustered and all of us late. There won't be much time to check in at the airport.

What I've been counting on is the airport being busy – and it is. It's far too small for all the arrivals and departures and the air conditioning's failed so everyone's really hot and bothered. The parents of the other holiday-making kids whisk them away in no time, but of course Bruce and I are still with the party when they start to queue for check-in.

'We don't seem to have a contact phone number for either of your parents – I can't understand it.' Miss Gumn swigs at her bottle of water.

'Mine are hopeless with mobiles,' I say. 'Probably didn't even bring theirs with them.'

'Same with mine,' Bruce says. 'Technophobes, both of them.'

I can see it's on the tip of Miss Gumn's tongue to say 'how irresponsible,' or something similar.

We're edging up to the point of no return. I've been scanning the crowds and at last I see what I've been searching for.

'There they are!' I yell. 'Look, Bruce, over on the far side.'

'Where? Oh yeah. I see them. 'Bye, miss. And thanks.'

'Yeah, thanks, miss. We'll be OK now.'

'Well, if you're sure...' She doesn't sound convinced. 'They're supposed to speak to a member of staff...'

'No time,' I say. 'Come on, Bruce.'

And we run towards a somewhat startled pair of middle-aged couples outside the coffee shop. Just before we reach them, I turn and wave to Miss Gumn. She waves, then turns back and is gone.

'Made it!' I say. 'We made it, Brucie Boy.'

He grins. 'Let's have a coffee, then we can get going.'

'It'll be expensive here. We better go and get on a bus – there's one that goes to Aggy Yarney quite regularly – it's really not too far from Gran's.'

An hour later and we climb off the bus. Our luck has been brilliant. But everything's about to change.

We're only about three miles from my grandmother's house but in this heat, that's a very long way. Afternoon is giving way to evening, but you wouldn't know it, the sun is as strong as ever.

We trudge along the dusty road, flanked by an olive grove on our right and a meadow full of withered grass on our left.

I wish we'd had the sense to buy some more water at the airport; we're both getting dehydrated and my head's beginning to throb.

'What is that noise?' Bruce gasps, as we toil up yet another hill.

'What noise?' I reply irritably.

'Like chips frying.'

I stop for a minute and listen – the air shimmers thickly around us.

'Cicadas,' I say at last. 'Is that what you mean?'

'What are – sickharders?'

I'm surprised he doesn't know. 'Like crickets,' I say. 'If you creep up on them, you can get a good look. They're all over the trees, but they're quite hard to spot.'

'Why would anyone want to?' Bruce says crossly.

I look at him. 'Aren't you interested in insects – natural history and stuff?' I ask.

'God, no. Whatever gave you that idea?'

I don't know. I really don't.

'I think I've got one can of Coke left,' he says. 'Wanna share?'

We climb down into the shade of a black cypress tree and flop down.

'How much further?' Bruce moans.

'Not much – I think. I've never actually walked it before.'

The Coke is warm and not even slightly thirst quenching.

Bruce closes his eyes and leans his head against the tree trunk.

'If you go to sleep,' I say, 'it'll steal your brains.'

'Sez who?'

'It's a well-known fact – well, a legend anyway.'

'Probably invented by some capitalist – a Greek version of Hamish – who wanted to make sure his workers didn't sleep on the job.'

'Got anything to eat?' I'm thinking, maybe something like an apple would be better than warm Coke.

I reach into the side pocket of his rucksack and my fingers close on something flat and squarish. Puzzled, I pull it out, expecting – maybe – an AfterEight mint. It's a packet of condoms.

CHAPTER TWENTY-ONE

Bruce opens his eyes, about to say something. Then he looks at me, then at the condoms, and back at me and finally at the ground, taking an apparently uncharacteristic interest in the progress of a line of ants.

'What's this?' I say, stupidly, at last.

'You know what it is, surely.' He sounds sarcastic.

'Taking rather a lot for granted, weren't you?'

'I – what can I say? I didn't know what might happen.' Now he sounds embarrassed. I want to crawl away into the tree roots. How toe-curling is this?

'I'm sorry,' he says, 'if they seem – inappropriate.'

I stand up abruptly. 'I'm going over there,' I say. 'I might be able to see a quicker way to Gran's down through those olive trees.'

'Emma?'

'Yes?'

'Nothing. Shout – if you see a path.'

I stumble away, face burning, brain racing. The olive trees give cool shadows, a welcome darkness. I go a few steps further and suddenly, far below, is a soft gleam and shimmer of sea. To the left I can see the village with Gran's house next to the small church, to the right the ribbon of road disappears upwards, twisting into the mountains.

The ground falls away steeply here, the olives thinning out rapidly. It should be possible to scramble down, cutting our journey in half. I turn round to call for Bruce and, as I do so, a large, pale-skinned gecko whizzes across my foot, startling me with its silent flight.

Then I'm falling, flying, tumbling. My hands are up to

protect my face but I can still see the world, blue and green and brown and gold as it revolves crazily around me. Everything happens in slow motion. I don't feel afraid, just curious to know what happens next. I can smell wild herbs, hot earth and the sea. Then there's a bump and blackness.

I open my eyes. My head hurts, so I suppose I can't be dead. All I can see is a blurry red light – it's coming towards me, then it swerves around me and screeches to a stop. I'm lying on my side. I try to sit up, and – apart from scratches on my arms and legs and the searing pain in my right ankle that screams 'Don't!' I seem to be more or less intact. Then a shadow falls across the sun. A man stands over me; he's saying something in Greek. I don't think I can remember any Greek, but out of nowhere I dredge up something which roughly translates as:

'I am English. I have an infection. I cannot speak Greek. I have fallen up the mountain.'

The man gazes at me for a second, then he starts laughing.

He offers me a hand. 'Can you stand?' he says in English.

'Sorry – I think so. My foot hurts.'

'What about your head?'

'That hurts a bit too. I think I passed out.'

'Passed out?'

'Unconscious.'

He nods. 'Come over here, sit down in the shade. I have some water.'

I do as I'm told. It's only when I've finished glugging about half a litre that I look at him properly. I must have banged my head harder than I think – he looks exactly like a young John Travolta. He speaks English with a slightly strange accent, part American, part Greek.

'You're English, right?' he says.

'Half English, half Greek – I'm Emma.' I offer him my hand,

116

see how grubby it is, and hastily withdraw it, wiping it on my shorts.

He smiles. Mr Seriously Gorgeous; bump on the head or no bump on the head. He's wearing a close-fitting white T-shirt, aviator-style shades tucked into the neck, and white chinos.

He's dazzling in more ways than one, about twenty-two or twenty-three, maybe, with the most amazing blue eyes.

'I'm George.'

'Thank you for picking me up off the road.'

'I nearly drove the car over you – you scare me. Are you on holiday here? Where are your family?'

And suddenly I'm telling George everything. Not quite everything, I don't tell him about Dad's court case. Just about coming here with Bruce to escape a potentially deadly summer.

He seems to understand, despite my gabbled English, smiling and frowning in the right places, listening patiently.

'So where is – Bruce – now? You said "Bruce" right? Like Bruce Willis?'

I giggle; suddenly, inexplicably, feeling much better.

'Nothing like Bruce Willis…He should be just off the road, up there,' I gesture vaguely. 'Unless he's come looking for me by now.'

He jumps up and once again offers me his hand. This time, I don't want to let it go, though of course I do.

'My car's not far. Let's go find him.'

Strangely, I don't hesitate. I don't think at all about the potential dangers of getting into a car with a guy I've only just met. Already, I feel sort of safe with him.

We climb into his car. It's one of those Suzuki Jeep things, very cool.

'Where are you staying?' he asks, starting the engine.

'With my grandmother – I hope. She lives here.'

'Here? In this village?'

'Yes. Perhaps you know her? Persephone Xenos?'

He looks startled. 'Persephone? But she's my godmother.'

We stare at each other. Being someone's godparent is a big deal in Greece. Why have I never heard of this guy?

'How come we've never met? Do I know your parents?'

'My mother,' he says quietly, 'she left me when I was a baby – ran away and never came back. And I never really knew my father.'

'So who brought you up?' I ask. 'Not Persephone – otherwise I'd know all about you.'

'I was sent away, to join the diaspora in the USA. I have cousins in New York. My father, he gave me his name, but nothing else.'

'Why didn't anyone tell me about you? Did you know about me?'

He smiles sadly. 'No one was proud of what my mother did, leaving me. It was probably easiest not to talk about it. Out of sight, out of mind... Yes, I know about you. Persephone often speak of you.'

'She does?'

'For sure.'

'Do you live here? Now?' It feels like I'm giving him the third degree, but I'm really interested.

'Yes. I came home about three years ago.'

With a sinking feeling, I realise he must know all about Dad. I realise too that if I'd been allowed to come to Kalos for the trial instead of being forced to stay in Wandsworth, I might have met George then.

As if reading my mind, he says quietly, 'You have another reason, for coming here this summer?'

I nod, dumbly. 'I want to find out the truth, to clear my father's name.'

He hesitates. 'You might find the truth hurt.'

'Let's go find Bruce,' I say.

We find him easily enough. He's asleep under the cypress tree where I left him. George sounds the horn and Bruce wakes with a start, staring uncomprehendingly at the pair of us in the Jeep.

'You should be careful. Those trees cannot be trusted – they take away your mind while you dream!' George laughs.

Bruce comes towards us, looking cross. I make the introductions, explain about my fall.

'It was OK,' I say. 'No biggy.'

'She might have been seriously hurt, even dead,' George says. 'You fell a long way.'

'At least you were around to pick me up.'

'Have you got any water?' Bruce croaks. 'I feel like I've been walking through the Sahara desert for several days.'

'Sure.' George passes him a fresh bottle. 'Where to now?'

'Gran's house, please,' I say.

He looks at me. 'I can take you there,' he says, 'but Persephone is gone.'

For one awful, gut-wrenching moment I think he means she's dead.

'Gone where?' Bruce asks.

'The mainland. I think she come back next week.'

I feel tears prick the back of my eyes. 'What are we going to do?' I whisper. 'We were counting on staying with her.'

'I told you,' Bruce says angrily. 'I told you to get in touch with her before we came.'

'And risk her telling Dad? Don't be stupid.'

119

We sit in silence, simmering for a moment.

George says, 'One of you can stay with me – I have a small room in the village. Maybe we can ask around for the other.'

Don't tempt me. But I can't just abandon Bruce.

'Thanks, George,' I say. 'But we can probably get into Gran's. There must be a key, and I'm sure she won't mind.'

George shrugs. 'Persephone is very – correct – she might think it not right for a boy and a girl to be alone together in her house, without her.'

'I'll risk that,' I say.

I find the spare key where it always is – under the terracotta pot with the faded dancing ladies around the rim.

Gran's had a shower put in since I was here last and it's blissful to stand beneath it, washing away the grime of the day. Bruce grumbles because I haven't left much water for him.

Later we meet up with George at the nearest taverna and eat fit to burst. There's a mixture of tourists and locals in the place. I recognise a few of the faces – Spiros the owner, his son Vassilis – but I keep my head down and ask George not to announce to everyone who I am. I'm too tired to cope with all that Greek curiosity tonight.

I'm relieved when no one comes up to George demanding to know who we are. George insists on paying and I agree, provided he lets us buy the meal next time. Bruce has chicken and chips, George and I have spit-roasted lamb that is totally delicious.

George drinks Mythos and Bruce and I drink Sprite. Afterwards we have strong black coffee. George smokes a lot. He has a way of holding his cigarette that makes me wish I did too.

We fall asleep between crisp clean sheets. Not only are Bruce and I in the same house but we're sharing a bedroom – though not a bed. Somehow neither of us wants to be alone tonight, and I wouldn't feel right sleeping in Persephone's room.

Before I turn out the light, I look across at Bruce.

'You OK?'

He nods. 'It's been a very long day.'

'And tomorrow's another one.'

There's a small silence.

'Emma?'

'Yes.'

'You notice how much George looks like John Travolta?'

So I'm not imagining it then. 'You think he tries to?'

Bruce snorts. 'You don't get hair like that by accident.'

CHAPTER TWENTY-TWO

'The question is,' Bruce says, 'where do we start?'

We're sitting outside, eating plump peaches from Persephone's tree for breakfast. Already, by nine o'clock, it's as hot as it ever gets at noon in England. Some of the cats have come to see us, rubbing up against our legs. We feel a whole lot better after a night's sleep.

'I have to go in the sea today,' I say. 'I just have to.'

'That'll be useful,' Bruce says. 'You're bound to find some clues there.'

I hit him.

'We'll talk to George later,' I say. 'Find out if he knew my other gran. That'll be a start.'

Somewhat to my surprise, Bruce doesn't want to come swimming.

'Not keen on the sea,' he says. 'Things live in it.'

'You're missing a treat,' I say. 'It's as warm as a—'

'Bath. Yes, Emma, I've read the travel brochures too.'

'Suit yourself.'

I leave Bruce reading under a fig tree and walk the few metres to the beach. I'm really pleased when I see George there, relaxing on a sunbed. His body looks toned and fit and oh-stop-it.

'Hi,' I say to George. 'Don't you have work to do?'

He jumps up immediately, insists I have the sunbed.

'I work mainly in the evenings,' he says, 'and today is my day off. I was coming to see you later.'

'What do you do?'

'All sorts of things. Sometimes I do Seventies nights karaoke, over in Aggy Yarney.'

'They pay you for that?'

'Sure. Why not? I'm very good.'

'I'm sure you are,' I say hastily. 'I didn't mean to be rude. It just seems a bit – unusual.'

He frowns. I'm beginning to get to know this frown. But I'm still not sure if it means he's cross or that he's having to concentrate to understand what I'm saying.

His spoken English is usually so good, I tend to forget it may not be his first language, despite his being brought up in America. He makes mistakes, more than Dino. Maybe the rellies who brought him up spoke Greek at home. I love his voice.

'I also do traditional dancing at the Aphrodite Hotel on Saturdays – folk dancing. And the other stuff depending on the audience.'

'Really?'

He nods. 'I do all sorts of things. Last winter I went back to the States and worked as a waiter. Sometimes I help out on the boat trips. I try to be – versatile.'

'Sounds good.'

'You should put some cream on – your skin will burn.'

'I didn't bring any stuff with me – I wasn't planning to stay, just go for a quick swim.'

'But you will burn fast. Here, I have some. Shall I put some on your shoulders anyway?'

I must have died and gone to heaven.

As he's massaging it in, he says, 'What about you, Emma? What do you want to do? You are leaving school soon?'

'Not very soon, unfortunately. I'm going to stay on and do A levels, then probably go to university.'

'And afterwards?'

'I don't know. I can't think that far. I used to think I'd like to

123

be a professional sax player, but I doubt I'm good enough or motivated enough – I haven't played for months.'

'You play saxophone? What music do you like?' He finishes and wipes his hands on his towel.

'Jazz, mainly.'

'Jazz? I love jazz, too – the old stuff, Miles Davis, so cool.'

'Sometimes I wish I could just take my sax and run away, live as a busker somewhere.'

'You stay at school, Miss Clever. You are lucky. I had to leave early – they wanted me earning money.'

'Bad luck,' I say. 'Would you have liked to go to college?'

He laughs. 'Maybe I would not have the motivation to work – but I like to have the opportunity.'

'Perhaps it's not too late, perhaps you could still go.'

He shakes his head. 'I need to earn money – and I like what I do now. You should come see my act – people say I do a good John Travolta.'

'Really? I'd never have guessed.'

'You're teasing me now. You don't think I look a little bit like John when he was younger?'

I don't want to look at his face, to gaze at that beautiful mouth, to drown in those blue eyes. 'Well, maybe just a bit,' I say.

After siesta George comes round and we sit in the cool stone-floored kitchen of Persephone's house, at the old pine table where I ate so many happy meals in my childhood. Bruce and I got some supplies in before lunch and now have enough bottled water to fill a swimming pool. It was hard work carrying it all home, but I didn't want to take advantage of the free delivery option in case people started asking questions, as no doubt they will, very soon. Gran's house is a bit away from the rest but it's not isolated. Someone will notice the unauthorised occupation – they'll probably think we're squatters and come round with shotguns.

George knocks the cap off a beer and lights a cigarette. Bruce coughs somewhat pointedly. I glare at him. George ignores him.

'What can I tell you?' George says to me.

'Firstly, did you know Susie Delacroix – my other grandmother who was murdered?'

He nods. 'I met her a few times. It's a small community, you know? She used to live close by, up in the hills.'

'Could she have had any enemies, d'you think?'

'Susie? No. She was friendly. She was a lady full of life: funny, young for her age. They say she had a little pain in the knees, from the running when she was a movie star, but that was all I think.'

'I'm sorry,' I say. 'We can't be talking about the same woman. Grandma Susie was old and quite frail. And she'd never been very sociable...'

'Who tells you this?' George draws on his cigarette.

'She was devastated when my mother died – it's why she cut herself off from my dad and me, why she never saw me when I came to Kalos. She was coming to England, to say goodbye to the old country. My father told me...They said it at the trial too.'

George looks out the window, clearly embarrassed. 'Only Dino say it, no one questioned it, no one asked anyone else, I think.'

'Are you saying her father lied?' Bruce says quietly.

George shrugs, one of those expressive Greek shrugs, then looks at his watch.

'Did you ever meet Susie's companion?' I say, changing tack.

'Companion?'

'Someone called Alexandra – she used to live with Susie.'

'Right. Yeah, I met her a few times.'

'What was she like? Do you have any idea why she left?'

He smiles. 'She was pretty, quite young, blonde hair, tall and strong – she needed to be to help your grandmother, I think. Perhaps somebody made her a better offer – it's not easy to look after old people, even when they are family and I think she was not of Susie's family?' He looks at me for confirmation.

I shake my head. 'Not unless she was a distant relative nobody knew about, and I don't think she was.'

'Some guy made her a better offer?' Bruce says.

'Maybe. There were some rumours, some gossip. Always people like to gossip.'

'Tell us,' I say.

But George shakes his head. 'I don't want to say bad things about anyone.'

I look at him, smile in what I hope is an irresistible way but is probably Wednesday Addams in concert.

'OK...But all I want to know really is: do you think this Alexandra had anything to do with Susie's death?'

'The police didn't think so. What could be the motive?'

'Perhaps she didn't want Susie to go back to England, or to change her will so that Dino got everything?'

'Dino or not Dino – either way, she got nothing – that's right isn't it? Like I say, no motive.'

We sit in silence for a few moments.

'I'm sorry,' George says at last. 'I have to go now, to see someone. Why don't you come see me do my act tonight?'

Dumbly, we nod our heads.

'I'll pick you up at seven.'

After he's gone I start to cry; not huge sobs, just fat tears running, almost silently, down my face.

'Don't, Emma.' Bruce tries to hug me. 'Please don't.'

But I feel as cold as ice and I can't respond, except with more tears.

'It doesn't mean anything,' Bruce says. 'He probably didn't know her very well – or maybe he knew her before she got sick.'

I wish I could believe that.

Bruce wants to paint some views in the village, particularly the small harbour next to the main beach. I know we should be making a start on what we came here for, but I guess we need to take time out to adjust to just being here alone; together.

Now he's off doing some sketching and I feel inspired to write poetry. I'm lying face down on a rag rug in Persephone's garden, watching an enormous bee buzzing among the tall plants – they could do with watering, but water's precious here.

Persephone has a well, maybe I'll draw some up later... Later, when I've stopped thinking about his beautiful mouth and the way his grey/blue eyes crinkle at the corners when he smiles. His shoulders are narrower than John's, but he has the same dimpled chin.

There must be about seven or eight years between us, I suppose. Is that too much? He's bound to think so. But then I remember Surrinder and Jas and the age gap between them. Maybe it won't matter, maybe he won't think I'm just a silly kid.

I'm excited about seeing George do his thing tonight in Aggy Yarney. (Its real name is Agios Ioannis, but locals and tourists alike call it Aggy Yarney.) I wish I had something good to wear...

While Bruce is having a shower I nip out to one of the tourist shops and spend some precious cash on a little strappy dress.

It's red and pink and gold and, though I say it myself, I look quite good. I can't do much with my hair. I apply some eye shadow and the ancient and hardly-used mascara I brought from home. Bruce comes out of the shower, rubbing his hair dry with a towel.

'You look – different,' he says.

Inside, the club is hot and steamy. George has gone off to change and Bruce and I sit at a small table drinking Coke, trying not to gulp it, to make it last.

I'm quite well aware that Bruce didn't want to come here tonight. Perhaps he's beginning to sense how I feel about George, though I've truly tried to hide it. The last thing I want is to hurt Bruce.

Then George appears – with two girls. One thinks she looks like Madonna and the other one actually does look like Olivia Newton-John in *Grease*. They both seem to be all over George and I'm so jealous I can taste it.

George's act is amazing – he wears a white suit for the *Saturday Night Fever* stuff and his dancing is really good. Then he and 'Olivia' do two numbers from *Grease*: 'Summer Nights' and then, after a quick costume change, 'You're The One That I Want'. I'm so enthralled by the performance that I don't notice Bruce. He's slumping further and further into his chair. George brought us over a trayful of cocktails in the break. I only notice the state Bruce is in when I go to start on my third.

'Are you OK?' I ask, unwilling to drag my eyes away from George for a second.

'No,' he says thickly. 'I think I'd better go home.'

'How? It's too far to walk.'

'Taxi. I'll ask the guy at the bar to get me one. You can stay, if you like.'

'Would you mind?' What a cow I am.

He shakes his head. I come with him to the bar and the taxi arrives shortly after.

'Sure you'll be OK?' I say, praying he'll say yes.

'Yes. See you later. Just need some air, really.'

When I get back to the table someone on stage is doing Elvis – there's no sign of George. Then I realise it is George. He really is versatile.

The show's over and I'm beginning to wish I'd gone home with Bruce when I had the chance. Not because it would have been the right thing to do, the thing you should do when a friend feels bad, but because George is virtually ignoring me. He's with a bunch of friends, men and women. 'Olivia' has her head on his shoulder and they're gabbling away in Greek so fast I can hardly catch a word. It's no use pretending I'm anything other than a stupid kid. How could I think I'd ever stand a chance with someone like George?

At last it's time to go. 'Madonna' and I get in the back and 'Olivia' gets in the front. Somewhat to my surprise we stop outside an apartment block after ten minutes and both girls get out of the car.

'Goodnight,' they say. (To George. I'm just the Invisible Girl.)

'Come in the front with me,' he says when they're gone.

I do as I'm told and we drive slowly home. The moon's up and it shimmers on the surface of the flat sea. We catch glimpses of silver as he guides the car skilfully round the bends.

'Did you like the show?' George says, steering with his knees while he lights a cigarette.

'It was great,' I say. 'And you were fantastic – especially when you did John Travolta – you're wasted here.'

'I think soon an agent will find me better work. I could be a – what is it?'

'Lookalike?'

'That's right – open shops, go to movie premieres, that sort of thing.' He smiles. 'I'd really like to act, you know? But as myself, not because I look like someone else.'

All too soon we're outside Persephone's house. He turns off the engine and we get out of the car. He yawns and stretches.

'Would you like to come in?' I say. 'Coffee?'

He shakes his head. Of course not – why would he?

'Are you tired?' he says suddenly.

'No – not really.'

'Then shall we walk, on the beach? I could do with some fresh air.'

We take our shoes off and walk on the sand. It's cold now of course, silky between our toes. It's way past midnight. The moon lights our way, making the beach clean and perfect.

'Is Olivia your girlfriend?' I say out loud. Why, I don't know.

He laughs. 'You mean Anna? No. We work together sometimes, that's all.'

'She's very good.'

'Yes. Her voice is not great but she dances like a dream.'

Then he takes my hand. We're walking along the beach together, holding hands. I feel charges of electricity running up my arm. We walk in silence towards the harbour.

'You look lovely tonight,' he says quietly. 'So different from when I pick you up from the road.'

'Thank you.' I don't know what else to say.

He stops walking and looks at me, asking a question with his eyes.

I nod, just a small incline of the head.

Then he kisses me, very slowly, and I'm drowning, drowning in the soft sweetness of his lips. He pulls me down on the sand and I want him so much. Fear and desire battle it out. Fear is retreating fast.

'You're so beautiful', he whispers into my neck. 'So sweet and beautiful. I want to make love to you.'

I kiss him harder. Then suddenly he breaks away and sits up.

'But not here,' he says. 'Here is not right. I want it to be perfect. Can I come to your house – to Persephone's house?'

'No!' I say, suddenly horrified. 'What if she came back? Anyway Bruce is there.'

He sighs. 'Of course. I wasn't thinking. Will you come to my room then? Thursday night? I don't work Thursday.'

Suddenly I'm not so sure, but I tell myself not to be a wimp. I smile at him.

'Yes, John.' Oh hell. 'Sorry, I mean George.'

'You call me John, if you like.'

Somehow I don't think I will. That would be a bit creepy.

We have one more long, slow delicious kiss.

'Until Thursday,' he says.

Can I wait that long?

When I tiptoe into the bedroom, Bruce is fast asleep. I feel his forehead – it's cool and he's smiling in his sleep. I fetch him a glass of water in case he wakes in the night feeling thirsty – like that makes my behaviour all right.

'Sweet dreams,' I say softly. 'I'm sorry, Bruce.'

But I'm not; not really. I can't be sorry about the way George makes me feel.

CHAPTER TWENTY-THREE

It isn't that I've forgotten why we've come. I suppose it's because I'm afraid that the truth I might find out isn't the truth I want to hear. And it's so easy on Kalos just to forget everything.

Bruce nods when I tell him this. He's been a bit subdued since last night. We're eating a hunk of delicious fresh bread with olive oil and drinking some very strong coffee on the paved terrace.

'*Kalimera!*'

An old woman walks across the garden. We both stand up but she waves us to sit down. I've seen her around the village, I think.

'You are Persephone's granddaughter,' she states, spreading her skirt and sitting down with us.

'Yes – I'm Emma – and this is my friend Bruce. But how did you know?'

She takes my hand in her old, brown wrinkled one.

'You look just like her.'

'No one's ever told me that before. I always thought I looked like my mother – English.'

She laughs, a high-pitched cackle. Bruce and I glance nervously at each other. The fact that she's dressed entirely in black enhances the witch-like effect.

'You are Greek, of Kalos; anyone can see that,' she says.

'Would you like some coffee?'

She nods.

'Have we met before?' I ask. 'It's a long time since I was last here.'

'When you were small. My name is Maria. Persephone is my good friend. I used to live on the other side of the island.'

'Do you know when she'll be back?'

'Next month, perhaps.'

'Next month? We thought she was only gone until next week.'

'She has friends on the mainland and business to do. I think next month she will return, or maybe later.'

'Oh.' My eyes fill with tears.

'Eh,' she strokes my hair, the rough skin on her fingertips brushing against my forehead. 'Why so sad?'

I tell her how we can't wait that long, how we have to get back to England. 'And I really wanted to see her again, so much.' I hadn't realised quite how much, until now.

'You are Dino's daughter.'

I nod, bracing myself for rejection. It doesn't come.

'He was a good man,' she says. 'Such a pity.'

'Maybe you knew my grandmother – I don't mean Persephone, I mean Susie Delacroix, the one who died?'

She nods slowly, thoughtfully. 'I knew Susie.'

She pronounces it 'Shooshy.' I think she has false teeth and maybe they don't fit so well.

'What was she like?'

'Well...' She rocks back in her chair, spreading her legs. 'More coffee?'

'Of course,' I say. 'Excuse me.' I find some delicious little almond biscuits in a tin too.

After her second cup she says, 'It isn't right, to speak ill of the dead, but Susie was a hard woman to understand. She liked to make people dance – like puppets you know?'

'Manipulative?' Bruce says.

Maria nods. 'That's it. Then of course she was ill for a long time and she got bad, in the head.'

*

133

After she's gone, Bruce says, 'So who's right about your grandmother – George or Maria?'

'Maybe they're both right, in a way – though I think what
Maria said sounded more convincing, even if it wasn't very
nice.'

'I'd tend to agree with you,' Bruce says.

'I suppose that means George is either mistaken ... or lying.'

'I'm sure there's something he knows that he didn't tell
us ...'

'But why? I say. 'What could he be hiding?'

'We should try to find that photographer, the one who
discovered the body,' Bruce says later, as we stroll down to the
harbour to take a look at the fishing boats. 'He was a key
witness at the trial – what was his name?'

'Costas Constantinos. He lives in Kalos town – that's quite a
big place. Don't know how we'd find him,' I say doubtfully.

We get the bus into Kalos town anyway. (Bruce, ever the
gentleman, gives up his seat to an old lady holding a baby goat,
whose undoubted cuteness fails to compensate for its appalling
smell.)

When we arrive at the town square we head for the tourist
office and fate smiles upon us. There, staring out at us from
the window, is a huge poster of a spectacular sunset, more
reminiscent of Armageddon than Kalos. On it, in three
languages, are the words: 'COSTAS CONSTANTINOS –
STARS AND SUNSETS. Photographic Exhibition at The
Museum of Modern Art.'

'Lead on, Sherlock,' says Bruce.

He seems in a better mood today, despite the heat and dust
of the busy town where the cars idle fretfully in the slow-
moving streets.

Chapter Twenty-four

We find the museum easily. I feel rather pleased with myself, as it's such a long time since I was last here. The interior is cool and perhaps because of that there are several people moving around among the exhibits. We follow the signs to Costas's exhibition. Not many people in this section: an old woman, a middle-aged couple and a man behind a desk whispering into a mobile phone. We pick up a catalogue and wander around the collection until he's finished his call. There are some stars, mainly in the shape of minor celebs, some paparazzi-style, some posed for, most of whom I don't know, but among those I recognise are Paris Hilton, Joan Collins, Nicolas Cage and John Hurt. Also, somewhat bizarrely, Tony Blair on a donkey. The sunsets are mostly taken on Kalos and other Greek islands, not especially inspiring but the sort of thing that's 'quite nice to have above the mantelpiece', as my Aunt Chris would no doubt say.

The man behind the desk finishes his call and looks up. We walk over to him.

'We'd like to see the photographer,' I say abruptly.

The man is small and round and sweaty and his curly black hair glistens when he turns toward the light. His teeth are brown.

'If you want to buy prints, make a note of the numbers and bring them to me.'

'Are you him?' Bruce asks.

'Who wants to know?'

'I do, I want to know. I'm Emma Xenos – you found my grandmother, Susie Delacroix, at the bottom of a cliff.'

His expression softens. 'Yes. I found the poor lady.'

'Could we talk to you about it? Please?'

'I already tell the police everything.'

'Please – it's important to me.' I smile. Wednesday Addams on acid.

'OK, but not for long – I'm very busy man.'

Busy doing what? I wonder. Certainly not selling many of his photographs.

'Come,' he says. 'We go somewhere.'

Bruce and I look at each other and he nods. This guy seems a bit creepy, but he's probably not dangerous. Anyway, there are two of us. He leads us up some stairs and suddenly we're out on a flat roof terrace, it's only a short flight, but Costas is wheezing and panting.

There's an amazing view of the harbour. Old fishing boats jostle democratically with sleek yachts and swanky Sunseekers in the greenish water. A ferry comes in from the mainland.

'Don't go too near the edge,' Bruce warns. 'It doesn't look very safe.'

Costas laughs, like a dog barking. 'Sit,' he commands, indicating some sun-bleached plastic chairs, hotter than a radiator on the backs of my legs.

He lights a cigarette. He tells us how he found Susie, what a shock it was, how he lost his camera ... give or take the odd word, it's exactly the same as the transcript of Dino's trial.

'What did you think?' Bruce asks him. 'What did you think when Susie said "Dino"?'

Costas looks at me. 'I think she meant to say Dino killed her.'

'Couldn't she have been calling for Dino to help her?' Bruce says.

Costas shrugs, a very Greek shrug. 'You think that if you like. Me, I don't think so.'

'She said something else, before she died?' I ask.

He frowns. 'I don't remember – yes, I do! She said "sand".'

'Why did she say that, I wonder?' Bruce scratches his chin.

Costas raises a finger towards his head, then thinks better of it.

'There was a lot of sand about,' he says.

That night I can't sleep. We're missing something, I just know it.

The next morning Maria comes again, this time bringing us some tomatoes and figs from her garden. After thanking her, I get down to business. I need to know about Susie's friends – and her enemies.

'Maria, did you know the lady who lived with Susie?'

It doesn't seem likely, but as Bruce said when we discussed it late last night, we have to explore every avenue, however unpromising.

But to my surprise, Maria is blushing. 'I – yes, I know her a little.'

'What was she like?'

'A tall girl, big and strong – with hair like corn.' She mutters something in Greek.

'Sorry, I didn't catch that.'

'I don't like to say, in front of your friend.' She nods towards Bruce, who's looking as bewildered as I am.

'Perhaps you could make some more coffee?' I say to him.

'I'd rather have water. It's too hot for coffee.'

I glare at him; how can he be so dense? Suddenly he understands.

'Won't be a minute,' he says.

He disappears into the house, but still Maria looks uncomfortable.

'Please tell me what you know,' I say. 'It might be important.'

She rocks back in her chair then forward, bending close to me as if there might be eavesdroppers in the vicinity.

'I never see this myself,' she says, 'but they say it's true.'

I can hardly contain my impatience.

'What do they say?'

'One day, Nikos, the man who delivers for the supermarket, a good man, his grandmother and I know each other many years . . . Nikos is married to Tsambika, she is from Rhodes and they have three fine sons—'

'What about Nikos?' My fingernails are digging into my palms.

'I was just about to tell you,' she says reproachfully.

'I'm sorry, please . . .'

She sighs. 'Nikos, who, as I say, is a man to be trusted. He is up at Susie's house delivering wine and ouzo and too much drink for an old lady, plus also some milk and cheese . . .'

She tails off. Please let her not be trying to remember what sort of cheese.

'Yes?'

'Mozzarella cheese, not local . . . anyway, he has to take the big van which don't fit up her little road so he has to walk from Stavros's place, so they don't hear him coming; anyway they have crazy loud old English music playing . . . and as he passes the window he sees her.'

'Who?'

'Alexandra. She is kissing someone.' She wraps her arms around herself, rocking, licking her lips. 'Very passionate, like this.'

It's hard keeping a straight face. Bruce has crept up behind her to listen.

'Who was she kissing? Did Nikos know the man?' I ask.

'No.'

'Oh . . . well, never mind.'

'There was no man,' she says, triumphantly.

'What do you mean?'

'That Alexandra was kissing your grandmother – like that!'

My grandmother, the lesbian. Well, life is full of surprises. I don't like to think too much about old people and sex – and old people and gay sex seems even worse, though, as Bruce points out, there's no logical reason why it should. Anyway, it certainly means that Alexandra might well have not wanted her 'lover' (eeuch!) to leave the island, might have been jealous enough to kill her.

I track down George. He's drinking a Mythos on the terrace overlooking the sea at Spiro's taverna. Bruce didn't want to come, says he has a headache. But he agreed with me that I should ask George if he knew about the true nature of the Susie/Alexandra relationship.

George listens carefully while I relate Maria's tale. He's smiling, trying not to laugh.

'It's not that funny,' I say. 'Actually, it's quite disturbing for me.'

'I'm sorry.' He looks at me, touches my hand and I melt, all I really want at this moment is to be kissing him, not sitting here discussing my late grandmother's sexual orientation.

'I did know,' he says softly. 'I never saw them together, but I heard the gossip. I nearly told you this the other day, but it didn't seem right – I didn't know if it was true.'

'Do you think Alexandra might have killed Susie, out of jealousy?'

He's silent for a moment. 'I suppose it's possible – though the police didn't think so. As far as I know, they never even suspected her.'

'No one could find her,' I point out.

There's a small silence, then George says gently, 'Are you still coming to see me on Thursday?'

'I'm not sure—'

He leans forward and brushes my lips with his.

'Yes,' I say.

He gets up and rummages in his pocket for some change to leave on the table. 'I have to go now. Anna needs to see me – some change to the act.'

I really hope that's all she needs to see him for.

CHAPTER TWENTY-FIVE

Persephone arrives home the next morning. Maria has been in touch with her.

I am so glad to see her. We both cry as we hug each other. Bruce smiles at us both, a little embarrassed.

'Why didn't you tell me you were coming, foolish one?'

Bruce goes off, to the internet café, he says, though I think he's just giving us some space. Persephone and I sit in the shade, shelling peas. There's a cat on my lap, warm from the sun.

'How come no one ever told me about George?' I say suddenly.

'George?'

'George. Your godson George. We've spent some time together since we've been here.'

'You have? Well – what should I tell you? He lived in America most of his life.'

'Yeah, I know that now. But before now I'd have liked to know about his existence at least. And I can't understand how his mother could just – abandon – him like that.'

She puts down the bowl, resting her hands on her knees.

'You must understand, she was very young, not much more than a baby herself.'

'So young she had to give him up?'

'She was thirteen years old.'

'Wow.'

'As you say. But it was a long time ago. The scandal was very bad.'

'So – how old is George now?'

She considers for a moment. 'Thirty-four.'

'That can't be right—' My voice trails away.

'That is right. I expect you noticed, he takes good care of

himself – he looks young for his age, I think.'

She looks at me keenly. 'Are you all right, Emma?'

'Yes. No. I thought he was younger, not much older than me.'

'He's just about old enough to be your father,' she says.

'You don't like him, do you? Why not? He's your godson.'

She picks up the bowl again. 'I don't like people who waste their lives. He had good chances in America. He has had a lot of help, money from his father's family, money from me. He has spent it all on nothing and still sometimes he comes back to ask for more. I tell him he should be ashamed, a man of his age...'

If Gran is shocked by our sleeping arrangements she doesn't say so. However she makes up a bed for Bruce in the sitting room just the same.

'You will feel cooler here.' She says it kindly. He smiles back at her, a little sheepishly.

Later on Bruce and I go for a walk up the dirt track that runs past Persephone's house. It's late afternoon and the heat has gone from boil to simmer.

'I still don't get it,' Bruce says. 'She must have meant something by it. People don't just say "sand" for no reason.'

'What though? It doesn't make any sense...not that we know if she had much sense by then.'

'I was thinking, maybe, she dropped something in the sand, some clue?'

'The police would have found it, surely.'

'Perhaps they didn't look, or they missed it – it's worth a try, isn't it?'

'We haven't any other leads, Sherlock. But when can we look? The place is full of tourists.'

'I suggest, Watson, that we inspect the scene at sunrise, before Joe Holidaymaker has had a chance to recover from the night before.'

The sunrise next day is truly awesome. The burning orange ball of the sun appearing over the horizon and lighting up the sea with fire. Soon it hurts to look at it and we have to get down to business.

'How do we do this?' I ask Bruce. 'I've only got a rough idea of where she fell.'

'We'll mark out the area, like they do on that *Time Team* thing. I've brought pegs and string; got them from the tourist mini-mart.'

'You're not just a pretty face, are you?'

He kisses me on the cheek. We've hardly touched since we arrived on the island, since I discovered the condoms, since I met George...

We mark out a large, squarish area.

'Of course,' I say, 'the sand could have shifted about quite a bit since it happened, we probably won't find anything. I still think the best plan is to track down Susie's girlfriend, if we can. I think it's highly suspicious that she vanished just a few days before Dino came, don't you?' I feel slightly sick, probably got up too early.

'Look at this rock,' Bruce says suddenly. 'It's so dark it almost looks bloodstained – I guess it's the mineral content... Emma? Are you all right?'

I'm not all right, I'm far from all right. The reality of it hits me for the first time. My poor grandmother, hurtling to her death, right here. Her blood on the rocks... her broken body on the sand.

I burst into loud, angry tears, surprising myself with the

ferocity of sudden grief for a woman I hardly knew. I sit on the ground, hugging my knees to my chest and howling like a baby. Bruce sits next to me, arms round me, I cry into his T-shirt, helpless, unable to stop. Eventually, after a few minutes, the tide recedes.

'Sorry,' I gulp, wiping my nose on the back of my hand.

'I'm sorry,' Bruce says, 'that wasn't a very sensitive thing to say.'

'It's just got real.'

'I know...do you want to go on? Or shall we give it up?'

'No way are we giving it up – we've hardly started.'

So we work our way methodically sifting and digging the sand. We have children's plastic rakes and spades rather than archaeologists' trowels, but we still manage to turn up a fascinating collection of cigarette ends, ring pulls, pebbles, shells, a crab's claw, a broken flip-flop and a rusty fork. By the time we've finished we're several centimetres down from the surface and tourists are appearing on the beach. The sunbed man is rearranging his wares for the day and the fruit man is chopping up wedges of watermelon with a terrifying machete.

'Let's go home,' I say at last. 'This is hopeless.'

It's Thursday at last. The awful thing is, I still want to see George tonight. Part of me wants to confront him and part of me, a very bad part, wants to forget how old he is and Persephone's judgement of his character. She could be wrong. She's quite conventional and George isn't, plus he spent most of his life in the States. Maybe she just doesn't understand him. Evening comes. Luckily Gran is tired and wants an early night, so it's easy for me to go out.

'I'm just going to take Maria's scarf back to her,' I say to Bruce. 'She must have left it here the other day.'

'I'll come with you.'

'Better not – if we both go she might keep us talking forever.'

'I'll go down to Spiro's then – maybe the internet café's still open.' He pauses. 'Meet you there in a while?'

'Sure.' I feel bad – but not bad enough to change my mind. I have to see George.

I walk slowly, enjoying the warmth of the evening. I hang Maria's scarf on the olive tree outside her front door and tiptoe away.

Then suddenly I'm almost running along the narrow road to George's house. It's not just that I'm longing to see him; an idea has come to me. I can't think why it never struck me before.

He's waiting for me. Wearing a tight black T-shirt that shows off his biceps and some even tighter Levi's.

'I hear Persephone is back,' he says, pouring me some wine. 'Does she know you come here tonight?'

'No. I didn't even tell Bruce.'

He smiles at me.

'She said some stuff, about you.'

'She has never liked me.' He sits next to me on the small sofa, his hand resting lightly on my knee.

'Why not?'

'Because I am not a lawyer or a doctor. Because I am free.'

'Was she right about your age?' I ask quietly. 'You're thirty-four – that's right?'

He shrugs. 'You're as old as you feel, that is what they say, isn't it?'

'You lied to me.'

'Lie? I didn't lie. You never ask how old I am.'

He's quite right. I didn't.

'I just thought you were younger, nearer my age.'

He smiles, that killer smile. 'I wish I was. Am I too old for you?'

'I don't know, part of me says "yes" – part of me doesn't care...but, anyway, there's something I have to tell you, something really important that's just occurred to me.'

'Yes?'

'We – Bruce and I, we went to see Costas. And he told us about finding Susie.'

'And?'

'He said, he said...' My heart's pounding, from the nearness of George or what I'm about to say I don't know. I take a deep breath. 'He told us Susie said "sand" before she died.'

'So? You knew that, from the trial I think?'

'Yes. But we thought it was about the sand, so we went to look where she – fell – and we didn't find anything—'

'Slow down, slow down, you go too fast,' he laughs.

'Sorry. OK. Anyway, I don't think she was saying "sand".'

'Well, what was she saying?'

'I think she was trying to say "Alexandra".'

George looks startled. 'You think?'

'Yes. It makes sense – more sense than "sand" anyway.'

'You know, you could be right.' He gets up and goes to the window. 'This changes things.'

'I know. It could mean that Alexandra killed her.'

'Yes...but it might mean that she was calling for Alexandra to help her. Anyway, you should tell the police – perhaps now they will find her.' His blue eyes gaze at me. 'You are very clever – what does Bruce think?'

'I haven't told him yet. I only thought of it on the way here.'

Suddenly his phone rings, making us jump. It plays a few notes of 'You're The One That I Want' from *Grease*, making me smile.

He answers, annoyed at being interrupted. And I don't care that he's thirty-four. I just want him. Now.

He gabbles something into the phone then ends the call. 'I'm really sorry, Emma, I have to go out.'

'Oh.'

'Don't look so sad. Will you come to me tomorrow?'

'Aren't you working?'

'Nope – or if I am I call in sick…kiss me goodbye, please?'

How can I resist? He wraps his arms round me and I lace my hands behind his head, wanting this, the sweetest of kisses, to last forever. It doesn't of course…but there's tomorrow to look forward to.

CHAPTER TWENTY-SIX

On the way home I meet Bruce. He might have been following me. I'm so excited that I tell him straightaway about my new theory. 'And George says we should tell the police.'

'When did you tell George?' he says quietly.

'I – just now. I told him just now.'

'What's going on, Emma? Between you and him – there's something...the way you look at him.'

I hesitate. 'He's thirty-four, Persephone told me.'

'That doesn't answer my question.'

But before I can think of what to say next, we've been joined by two large men.

'What the hell do you want?' Bruce says.

I can hear the wobble in his voice – I hope they can't.

'Come with us,' one of them growls.

And we're being frogmarched down the street. Why is there no one about? Where is everyone? I want to pee really badly. Then we're thrust into an open doorway and told to sit down.

'What have we done?' I ask. 'We were just going home to my grandmother...'

Another one says, 'This won't take long.'

And then Costas comes in, sits down heavily opposite us. The men melt to the corner of the room.

Bruce and I look at each other – what the hell is going on?

'I cannot sleep,' Costas tells us dramatically, wiping his sweaty brow with the sleeve of his jacket. 'It is a punishment I can no longer bear.'

Perhaps he's gone mad. Instinctively, neither Bruce nor I say anything. We avoid eye contact with each other and with Costas. We look at the floor.

'I had to tell you the truth, you see. I am sorry – I have been watching you since our meeting.'

'Why would you want to do that?' I risk a question.

'About your grandmother's death – there is something you should know. I must tell you now or never sleep again.'

'Go on.'

His eyes narrow. 'You must agree to do something for me in return.'

'I thought you wanted a good night's sleep.' I force myself to look directly at him, lifting my chin up, showing him I'm not afraid. Not sure he's convinced . . .

'Yes, I want to sleep. But still I want something from you – is only fair.'

'What is it you want?'

'A little thing . . . I only want to photograph you, on the beach, crying for your dead grandmother. I saw you but I didn't have my camera, otherwise I try then. But anyway is better if you agree – I can light it properly, take several shots.'

'Why? Why would you want that? I'm not a celeb.'

'There are people – people who would like to see anyone or anything that once belong to Susie Delacroix.'

'That's sick—'

I'm about to tell him exactly what I think of this idea when Bruce catches my eye. He nods his head, mouths 'yes'.

I take a deep breath. 'OK, I'll do it . . . But first you have to tell me, what's keeping you awake at night, Costas?'

He settles back in his chair, gets out a cigarette. 'OK. I tell the police that I find her, Susie Delacroix, that morning on the rocks, that I didn't know who she was. But that wasn't true. I knew who she was, I saw her with your father the night before. I knew who she was.'

'Why didn't you want the police to know that?' Bruce speaks.

'Because I am ashamed. I did nothing – I did something.'

'Well, what did you do, or not do?' I sit on my hands to still my impatience.

'I wait until your father go to the toilet, then I ask is OK for me to take a photo? She say no but I get my camera ready anyway, in case she change her mind. Sometimes they say no and they mean yes. Always I want a photo of Susie Delacroix and it makes me mad that she lives on my island yet I never see her. Once I write to ask if I can take some of her at home but she don't reply.

'So I go to the house and that woman, that Alexandra, shouts at me to go away. She chases me with a broom.'

'You might have got an interesting shot of them together, if you'd hung around,' Bruce says.

I flash him a warning look.

'So when I see Miss Delacroix that night I can't believe my luck. But she won't help me. Still, she say no. She gets up, hiding her face with her hands and she leaves the taverna. I follow, calling her name, but she never looks around. She start to run and I start to run but then I fall over a bloody dog and lose my glasses. When I find them again, she's nowhere – vanished. It's not possible . . . I think perhaps she's hiding, but there's only the old goat shed and she would not hide there.'

'Why not?' I ask.

'Dirty. Stinky, even though no goats for many years. It's not a place for Miss Delacroix.'

'So you think she may have run over the cliff, to get away from you?' Bruce says slowly.

'I think so. I think it's possible. You see now why I lied to the police and why I can't sleep.'

'How did she manage to outrun you, even for a little while? You're a lot younger.'

He clutches his chest. 'My heart is not so good. And you forget Susie Delacroix could once run like the wind.'

'OK, I believe you.'

'I suppose that means,' Bruce says, 'that she may have run into her killer after she got away from you.'

'Will you tell the police?' Costas's head is in his hands.

'Don't know. I'm not sure it makes a lot of difference – and we've actually got some other information that might change everything.' I stand up. 'Can we go now?'

'What do you have to tell the police that is more important than what I just tell to you?' He sounds almost disappointed.

'We can't say,' Bruce says. 'But I expect everyone will know, soon enough.'

'We do the photograph on the sand soon.' He stands up, hands me a card. 'You will call me to arrange?' he says.

'When hell freezes over,' I smile sweetly.

'What?'

'I'll call you soon.'

We leave the building and make our way quickly down the street, not looking back.

'What a weirdo,' Bruce says.

'Do you think he was telling the truth?'

'Difficult to say. He's the kind of guy, if the church clock struck twelve, and the speaking clock said twelve, and you asked him what the time was and he said twelve ... well, you'd begin to doubt it really was twelve.'

'I think we should write it all down, everything we think we know, then give it to the police as soon as we can. I think they need to try again to find this Alexandra.'

CHAPTER TWENTY-SEVEN

It's Friday afternoon and I'm drying my hair with a towel, thinking about tonight. After last night's disappointment I really want everything to be perfect.

'Do you want to go for a walk, now it's a bit cooler?' Bruce says.

'I – I might go see Maria.'

He turns without a word and is gone. I wonder whether gold eye shadow makes me look more sophisticated and ponder the advisability of flavoured lip gloss.

The time has come. Persephone's watering the garden and I shout a quick goodbye through the window. 'See you later, *Yaya.*'

I walk towards George's, knowing how momentous this night could be, longing to see him but a bit afraid – of myself and my feelings and where they might lead.

He opens the door to me and we kiss on the doorstep. Inside the soundtrack from *Saturday Night Fever* is playing. He takes me by the hand.

'Dance with me,' he says.

'I can't dance – not like you.'

'Sure you can.'

And he holds me close and we move to the music: 'How Deep is Your Love?'

Then his phone rings. I want to snatch it and throw it out the window.

'I'm sorry, Emma, I have to take this – I'll go outside, better reception.'

I can't help wondering if it's Anna/Olivia wanting to know why he's not at work.

He goes outside and I wander around, looking at his film posters, his costumes and wigs. I look again at the *Grease* poster of John and Olivia – Danny and Sandy.

Sandy?... Sandy?

Is it possible that Alexandra, my grandmother's mysteriously vanished companion, is none other than Anna/Sandy, George's dancing partner? But it can't be...

George comes back in suddenly.

'I'm sorry about that,' he says. 'Nick from work... you been looking at my costumes – they're good, aren't they?'

He moves to kiss me but I sidestep him.

'George – is Sandy gay?'

He smiles. 'Sandy? You mean Anna? I don't think so, but she flirts with everybody, boys and girls. Why do you want to know that?'

I don't answer him.

'Hey, are you jealous? You know she come on to me, but our relationship is strictly professional.' He takes my hands and pulls me toward him.

Anna can't be the Sandy who was with my grandmother, Anna is petite and quite delicate-looking. Alexandra, everyone seems to agree, was a big, strong girl.

'Why don't you kiss me? I know you want to.'

And amazingly I still do. I just can't help myself, or maybe I can't quite believe what's happening. I can't think straight... Can what I'm thinking be possible?

George smells of soap and some delicious herby fragrance. I run my hands through his hair. My fingers turn black. I don't notice this until I start pushing against his bright white T-shirt.

'I'm so sorry.' Inside I scream with embarrassment. 'I'm not sure I want to.'

He dyes his hair, or more likely sprays it black. Dye wouldn't have come off on my hands. 'I'm sorry about your T-shirt. Will it wash out?'

He says nothing, stalks off to the bathroom. When he returns he's wearing a fresh T-shirt with Elvis Presley's face on it. Underneath it says 'The King'. He pours himself a large Metaxa brandy and knocks it back in one go.

'You won't tell anyone about my hair.' It's a statement, not a question.

'Of course not – why would I? Anyway it's no big deal. Lots of guys dye their hair.'

'You still want to go to bed with me now?' He is being sarcastic.

I say nothing. What can I say? My heart's thumping and I feel a stupid urge to laugh – hysteria, probably.

'Why are you smiling – you think it's funny?'

Suddenly he hits me – wallop – on the side of my head. I'm so shocked I can't speak. In a daze I watch him pour another huge Metaxa and drink it in two gulps.

The ring on his little finger cut my cheek. I look at his hand and at the ring. I know it's not a man's ring. I know because I've got one just like it at home. Mine belonged to my grandmother Susie.

'Where did you get your ring?' I say pleasantly, like he hasn't just walloped me and I'm making polite conversation.

He looks at it as if for the first time. Then he smiles in a what-the-hell kind of way.

'I think you know where I get it.'

I can think of nothing to say.

He goes to the door and locks it. Now I'm afraid, now I'm very afraid.

'So you don't smile now.' Yet another brandy. Perhaps he'll

fall over in a minute. Please let him fall over.

'Did you take her ring? Or did she give it to you?' My head's telling me to say nothing, so why won't my mouth obey?

For a moment I think he won't answer, then: 'She cheated me, she tricked me. She promised me money if I took care of her. She said she'd make me a big star. She know people, show-business people.'

'What happened?' My voice is a whisper.

'She change her mind. She gets older and more cuckoo and says she wants her daughter's family to have the money. Why? She hasn't seen them for years. They don't care about her.'

I try to shrink into the sofa. Why is he telling me? He's not going to tell me and let me go, is he? If I can keep him talking, maybe the brandy will get the better of him. I can't believe what I'm hearing...

He continues, 'When I hear she going to England, I totally flipped.'

'How did you do it?' I ask, trying to keep my voice level.

He laughs. 'She phoned me on the last day to say goodbye. She told me she and Dino would go to the taverna that night. She asked me – told me – not to go. I went there and I see Dino give her pills. Precious bloody Dino who don't even speak to me in the street. The taverna is very busy, people to say goodbye to Susie, and someone else is having a name-day party also. I have to wait until nearly everyone go. I go too, but I stay close. Then when Dino goes to the john I call Susie on her cell, tell her to come outside, have a last drink, say goodbye. I tell her how I will miss her. She says she's had too much already but still she agrees. Only trouble is, that fool Costas follows her out, trying to take her photo. But then I get lucky, 'cos he fell over chasing after her and we hide away behind the old goat shed while he searches. We laugh – it's fun.'

He pauses, lighting a cigarette. 'Then we go for a little walk, just the two of us, nice and friendly. We go right to the old bench, where you can see the lights from the mainland – you know it?'

I don't, but I nod anyway, so as not to distract him. I realise that he's enjoying telling me this, that he's been bursting to tell someone for a long time...

'I have everything ready in my backpack – a bottle of Cair, nice and chilled, and two glasses. We toast each other. I try to get her to change her mind or at least give me some money. She owes me. But she won't, old bitch. She laughs at me, like I'm nobody... so I see no one's looking and I punch her – to teach her a lesson.'

He says this like it's a reasonable thing to do.

'Then I take the money in her bag – about two thousand euros – not so much. She starts to shout – she didn't learn the lesson. So I give her a little push and over the cliff she went. Bye bye, Susie.'

'Why didn't anyone suspect you? Didn't anyone see you?'

He laughs. 'That Susie, she want to keep our relationship quiet. She said I was her special secret. Special. And nobody ever know – she made me dress as a woman. When I live at her house I am Sandy, or Alexandra.'

'Why "Sandy"?'

'There was an English singer she like very much – Sandy Denny.'

'Creepy.'

'Creepy? No. It was fun ... Actually, I make a very pretty girl.'

Actually, I can believe it.

'You killed someone – for money?'

'There's a better reason to kill? They think that's why Dino did it – for the – inheritance – don't they? But I didn't mean to

– I lose my temper when she laughed at me – when I realise I mean nothing to her.'

I nod. 'But how could you be sure Dino would leave her on her own?'

He walks around the room, chest puffed out, still drinking, drawing deeply on his cigarette. How could I ever have wanted him? How could I have ever thought he looked like John Travolta? Now he just looks old and mean and so, so pleased with himself.

'I didn't know he would. But I thought he might.' He winks at me, like we're sharing a joke.

'Why?'

'I can't think of the English word – in Greek is: *kathartica*?'

'Laxative,' I say flatly.

'That's it.'

'I don't understand.'

'They have big night at Spiro's. I told you, many people are there, even me; though old bitch Susie pretends she don't know me. I got really strong laxative, and every time Dino's back is turned I put it in his food and his beer.'

'You bastard,' I say. Foolishly, as it turns out.

'Don't you call me that!' He slaps me across the head again, then pulls me to my feet. He stubs out the cigarette on the wall and it falls to the floor.

The next thing I know I'm flat on my back on his bed and he's on top of me, squashing the life out of me.

'I might not let you live.' He's stroking my cheek. 'But I can make love to you before you die. It isn't fair to send you to heaven without you know how good it is. I am a good lover, even though I drink so much.'

'Please don't,' I gasp. 'Please – I don't want to.'

'I know that. You think I don't know that? That makes it

157

better for you and for me. I never had a virgin.'

All the while his hands are groping me. Perhaps if I scream… That's a seriously bad idea. His hand clamps over my mouth like a door slamming shut. I can't breathe…I'm passing out…

CHAPTER TWENTY-EIGHT

There's a great hammering on the door, men bellowing – the most welcome sound in the world. Cursing in Greek, George stands up. Unbelievably, he's straightening his clothes, his hair.

'Don't you say nothing. I tell them you tried seduce me. They think you're a silly little slut. And if you tell about Susie I'll say you're lying too; say you're crazy. No one can prove anything, you understand?'

I nod. What else can I do? Then he's out the window and gone. And the door bursts open and Bruce and Spiro and two other guys from the village burst in, and Hamish. Hamish? I must be hallucinating. I try to tell them what's happened, but I'm not very coherent. The graze on my face hurts.

Then everyone's shouting and swearing and I sit in the corner, hands over my ears, eyes tight shut – until Bruce yells louder than anyone and tells them all to BE QUIET! Then they lead me away to Persephone's house and to sanctuary.

George doesn't get far, they catch up with him near the harbour.

So how does it feel to be the Stupidest Girl in the World? Not good, not good at all. No one has lectured me about the senseless risk I took when I went to see George alone. I almost wish they would. Instead they just look at me reproachfully.

Bruce is barely speaking to me and who can blame him? If I was him I wouldn't speak to me either. He did tell me that he knew he had to find me that night; he sensed I was in big trouble. And when he told Spiro where he thought I'd gone, Spiro couldn't recruit a posse from the bar fast enough. No one, it seems – except the Stupidest Girl in the world – ever liked or trusted George much.

And Hamish wasn't an hallucination. Seems Bruce and I had overlooked one little flaw in our cunning plan, which was that someone from the school might go into the shop while we were still in Kalos... Not just someone as it turns out, but Mr Hampton – who actually lives about a million miles from the school, as far from his pupils as possible. Of course Hamish mentions Bruce's extended trip to Rhodes to Hampton and the rest, as they say, is history – or maybe geography.

Hamish, who has never been out of the British Isles, hotfoots it to Kalos, tracks us down and is just in time to take part in the rescue of the Stupidest Girl in the World. He's the one, along with Spiro, who catches George down by the harbour. Amazing, considering his age. He gets lots of praise from the locals for his speed and courage.

'I've had many years of practice,' he says, 'chasing shop-lifters.'

Persephone and I have a little talk, the day that Bruce and Hamish fly home. Dad and Jan are coming to fetch me in a few days' time.

We're sitting under the grapevine in the garden, Bruce is packing. I'm holding some white wool, looped over my hands, which Persephone is winding into balls.

'So why did you come here, really?' she says, directly.

'To prove Dad's innocence, to find out what really happened,' I answer equally directly.

'Who did you need to prove his innocence to?'

'Everyone. Everyone who believed he did it.'

'But his name was already clear.' She takes up a jug. 'As clear as this water. He was Not Guilty at the trial – was he not?'

'You don't understand,' I say. 'That wasn't enough . . . people at school, the neighbours . . .'

She waves her hand, impatient, dismissive. 'There will always be ignorance. People like to gossip, and bad gossip is so much more interesting than good gossip. But all gossip grows stale, sooner or later.'

She pours me some water, then she says it: 'Was it, perhaps, to yourself that you needed to prove his innocence?'

'No! Absolutely not! I always knew he couldn't do it.'

But I know at last that she's right. And that makes me spiteful.

'What about you?' I say accusingly. 'Dino's your son – you thought he was guilty too, didn't you? What about that stuff in the newspapers?'

There's a pause while she puts the wool down.

Then she says, 'To my shame, I did. Not for long, you understand, not for more than half a day. It was because of the money, of course – so much money would be enough to tempt a saint. I foolishly spoke to someone who pretended to be a friend – a journalist.' She practically spits the word. 'She twisted what I said, changed it, made it backwards and inside out and just – wrong.'

'That's why we didn't come here any more.'

She shakes her head. 'No, Kyria Emma, that isn't the reason. The reason, as your father should have told you, is that he thought he'd brought shame on our family name, even to be suspected of such a crime. And he felt he was guilty, because he didn't take good enough care of Susie. If he had, she might still be alive.'

'You're right,' I say softly.

'Do you know what some people called me in the village?'

I shake my head, but I'm not surprised by the answer.

'They call me: "Murderer's Mother".'

'I'm so sorry,' I whisper. 'They called me: "Killer's Daughter".'

She shrugs. 'You must face up to these things, hold your head high. Here they soon got tired of it. And my good friends helped me. But now, I suppose, I must be "Murderer's Godmother" for a while – until they tire of that too.'

'Does everyone know? About George? How?'

She laughs. 'You can't squash a grape in this village without everyone knows. That's why I cannot believe no one knew about him and Susie. She was a clever one.'

'I could kill George,' I say fiercely. 'Bastard – sorry, Persephone.'

'He's been called worse than that – by me, for one.'

'One thing I don't understand – why did he lie to me about Grandma Susie? Making out she was fine before she died?'

'Who knows? He tells many lies. Maybe it was a – whatisit? – A "smokescreen". His whole life is a lie – pretending to be this Hollywood actor.' She sighs. 'I should have protected you more from George—'

I start to protest, but she holds up her hand to silence me.

'I still had faith in him, you see. Still hoped my good-for-nothing godson would do the right thing one day. And I didn't see how – infatuated – you were with him. As well I never thought he would go after a girl so young.' She shakes her head. 'You must be more careful of men, my Emma. You're growing into a very beautiful young woman.'

'Yeah, right,' I say.

She looks puzzled of course, but she doesn't pursue it.

I tell Bruce to blame the whole thing on me, so it's hardly surprising that Hamish forbids him to see me (again). But this time, Bruce obeys him.

I was expecting Dad to be really mad at me, but he's hardly said anything. When he arrived at Kalos Airport he hugged me like he'd never let go. I don't know how much Persephone told him. Jan's a bit distant, but then she's busy making plans for the new house. I get the feeling she may be distant for a while – and who can blame her? I lied to her, caused her all this anxiety. I tried to apologise, to make her understand why I had to come to Kalos. She changed the subject. I guess it'll take time to mend what I've broken.

EPILOGUE
AT LAST

The good news is that I don't have to go back to horrible Hillingbury High. The great news is that they've sent me to this boarding school in Kalos. It's called The Academy and there are people from all over the world here. They teach in English and you can do English, American or European exams. I'm thinking of doing something called the International Baccalaureate instead of A levels, when I've got through my GCSEs. I thought they'd all be a bit stuck-up, with it being a private school, but everyone I've met so far has been really nice. It's expensive, but, as Dino says, it's only for a few years.

The plan is that I'll spend some holidays with Persephone and some in France with Dad and Jan. The best thing is that Dad and Jan are coming to Kalos for two weeks in December and Persephone's going to cook the most gargantuan turkey of all time on Christmas Day.

I don't know what to say about Bruce except that I know I let him down badly. I could say it all started to go wrong between us when I discovered the condoms on that first day in Kalos.

The thing is I'm not sure that Bruce really wanted to go all the way with me either. Maybe he was just being a good Boy Scout: 'Being Prepared'. He's far more sensible than me, and who knows what might have happened in the romantic, sexy, night air of Kalos? Probably he was just as unsure as I was. I should have talked it through with him and maybe I would have done, if George hadn't become part of the picture.

*

It'll be a while until George's case comes to trial. I don't know if I'll have to give evidence. I don't know what the rules about that are here. George told the police that I was a silly little girl with a crush on him who couldn't handle rejection. Apparently I tried to get revenge when he turned down the offer of my virginity by making up ridiculous stories... Luckily, the people who matter to me know him for the liar he is.

He may think he'll get away with it but he's wrong. If the court doesn't punish him then I will. I don't know how I'll do it but one day I'll make him pay. It's a promise I make to myself and to my dead grandmother, who should have died peacefully between clean white sheets, not at the foot of a cold and lonely cliff at the hands of a psychopath.

Bruce emails me from time to time. This is his latest:

HI EMMA ! (I'm shouting 'cos ur sofa away)

The news here is that we had a talk from Hampton yesterday. He said that now we're Year 11s we must all keep our noses to the grindstone (you can guess what I said).

Megan Marsh is back at school. Apparently her own stepfather beat her up but she was 2 scared to say who it was – really bad thing. She's In Care now. I know she was a prize bitch 2U but you can't help feeling sorry for her.

What else? Soph's Doberman's had yet more puppies – Hamish is thinking of buying 2 as guard dogs as we had a break-in last week. You'll never guess what they took... Emma, don't even try to guess. They took the entire stock of cat food. Hamish had got loads of some special stuff for that mad Siamese woman.

He's been OK with me recently – thinks I'll be a good

165

boy now that ur off the scene and no longer able to influence me with your wicked wiles. (Yes. Yes he did actually say that). I've decided I'm going 2 art school after Hillingbury High, whatever Hamish thinks. We only get one chance at life, as my dear old mother is always saying.

Anything else? Oh yes, the school fish all died during the summer, Katie Cooper's pregnant, and I'm going out with Stacey.

BTW Hamish has a new ad in the window – I borrowed it to scan (attachment – I thought you'd like to see it, click on it now.)

I click. This is what it says:

HAVE YOU EVER WANTED A VERMINOUS PET? WE NOW STOCK GERBIL'S. THEY ARE NICE LITTLE FELLOWS WITH PLENTY OF CHARACTER KEEP YOU AND YOUR KIDDIES AMUSED FOR HOURS. WE HAVE EVER GERBIL NEED AND ~~ACKOOTR~~ ACCESSORY INCLUSIVE OF CAGES TOYS BEDDING AND OF COURSE THEY'RE ALL IMPORTANT FOOD. REASONABLE PRICES, BUY ONE GET ONE FREE. LIMITED OFFER. BOTH GENDER'S AVAILABLE.

Unfortunately (the email continues) the stock escaped and the Nice Little Fellows with Plenty of Character ended up decimating the Unrivalled Selection of Biscuits. Hamish put them in the bargain box (the biscuits, not the gerbils).

Stacey's yelling at me to come and admire some dress she's bought so I'd better stop now. Email me soon with news from Krazy Kalos. Byeeeeeee, Bruce. XX FRIENDS ALWAYS (I'm shouting because ur miles away).

Do I mind? Not about the gerbils, obviously. But yes, I do mind about Bruce and Stacey. But I know I have no right to. I'm miles away. We have to move on, both of us. At least I still have Bruce as a friend – and that's more than I deserve.

Things change, they change all the time. That's what Persephone once told me years ago, when I was unhappy about something. I can't remember what. They change whether you want them to or not. Sometimes you do and sometimes you just want everything to stay the same forever and ever. It makes no difference. Things change.

Tonight they're showing *Face/Off* at the school film club. John T AND Nicolas C. My cup runneth o'er, as some poet said.

Of course I wouldn't let George spoil John Travolta for me. When I'm watching John again I realise that, actually, George hardly looks like him at all. You can't fake style. You can't fake class. You can't fake the real thing.

I have my own room – actually it's not much more than a cubicle but at least I'm not sharing. On the wall is the beautiful painting that Bruce gave me for my birthday, a zillion years ago. From my window I can look down on a small courtyard in the centre of which is a simple stone fountain. It's very peaceful.

Someone – a tall, fair girl – comes up to me in the canteen.

'Your name's Emma Xenos, right?'

'Yes,' I say defensively. 'That's right. What about it?'

'Is it true your father is Dino Xenos?'

'Yeah, so?'

She thrusts her fist into my face.

'Look – he made this ring. You are so lucky to have such a father. Always I ask my father for jewellery for my presents and always he buys something of your father – it is a coincidence, no?'

And on and on she talks. Turns out her name is Inge, she's Swedish and she's new too.

They have a good system here, which is that there's a wall next to the entrance hall covered with photographs of all the students and teachers and a little bit of information about each. Anyone new (staff or student) is in a marked-off section in the middle under a sign saying 'WELCOME' in five different languages. The whole thing would last about five minutes in Hillingbury High before someone defaced it. But no one does here.

Under my photograph (artfully taken at sunset, me gazing soulfully into the middle distance). I've written:

'EMMA XENOS: – SAX PLAYER, LUNATIC –
JEWELLER'S DAUGHTER.'